Past Imperfect

Past Imperfect

Hilary Grenville

ROBERT HALE · LONDON

© Hilary Grenville 2000
First published in Great Britain 2000

ISBN 0 7090 6727 5

Robert Hale Limited
Clerkenwell House
Clerkenwell Green
London EC1R 0HT

2 4 6 8 10 9 7 5 3 1

Typeset by
Derek Doyle & Associates, Liverpool.
Printed in Great Britain by
St Edmundsbury Press, Bury St Edmunds, Suffolk.
Bound by Woolnough Bookbinding Ltd.

Chapter 1

What could have been more innocuous than my meeting with Jessica Hammond in the supermarket on that Saturday morning? There was no reason to anticipate trouble.

'Emma!' she called: a neat little figure, her big blue eyes and apparent fragility camouflaging her talent for carving a course through the tangle of trolleys and leaving a trail of staggered shoppers in her wake. 'When did you get back? I thought you were still at Martinsfield.'

'I was until a few weeks ago,' I said, 'but that project is finished. I'm giving myself a short break before going on to something new.'

'How could you bear to leave that dishy Maxwell North?'

I wasn't rising to that one. Maxwell, the owner of the house which had been the centre of my life for more than eighteen months, was a darling, but old enough to be my father. Dishy was definitely not the way I would describe him. Tall and powerfully built, conventional good looks had passed him by, but his dark eyes and heavy eyebrows and the unruly hair – more heavily streaked with grey than when I had first encountered him – all gave him a striking presence.

I had no intention of adding extra ammunition for Jessica's scandalmongering by revealing that Maxwell and I had recently returned from a couple of weeks at his place in Brittany . . .

although, I must admit it was tempting to allow her to build up her picture of debauchery, and then to mention casually that we had been more than adequately chaperoned by Maxwell's gem of a housekeeper.

Maxwell and I had – still have – great affection for each other, but our relationship is nearer father and daughter than lovers.

That break had been the culmination of a mixture of evil, tragedy, and terror, followed by the most absorbing and fascinating project when, as an architectural historian, I had been advising on the restoration of Martinsfield House and grounds, the run-down estate inherited by Maxwell. I would be back there again from time to time.

'How are you all?' I said, bypassing Jessica's question.

'Fine . . . except for Aunt Harriet. She really is with the fairies these days. She's talking such rubbish, and she seems scared of her own shadow – jumps at the slightest noise.'

I was sad to hear that bit of news. The description didn't seem at all like Harriet Travers, whom I remembered as an engaging character who had led an interesting life and, in her seventies, could still eclipse many half her age. Now, it sounded as though that could all be in the past.

The morning shoppers were getting a little edgy. We were blocking the supermarket aisle. It was no place for a chat.

'Come back for a coffee,' Jessica said. 'I'm on my own. The kids are away at school, and Barry is in New York on a business trip.'

Barry's absence accounted for her relaxed manner. I'd always considered him a bit of a pain. I had other plans for that morning, but for the sake of the marooned shoppers, I accepted the invitation.

'I'll just drop this lot at the flat first,' I said.

Half an hour later I arrived at the Hammond abode – a palatial pad with all the trimmings that prosperity can provide. Although

Barry never spoke about his work and, oddly enough, neither did Jessica, he was clearly doing very well.

I was parking in the drive when another car slid alongside. The driver got out and a once familiar face appeared at the window.

'Ah! The one that got away,' he said, eyeing me with mock sorrow.

I laughed. Jessica's brother, Peter Jackson, and I went back a very long way – to our school days, in fact, when we had been mutually attracted for all of six months. It was some years since our last meeting. He had gone through two marriages and the odd affair. His career had been equally patchy, and included a short spell in the army which, apparently, neither he nor the army had enjoyed. But, to Peter, any hitch presented a challenge and, if things went wrong, he always had the ability to bounce back. In a way, that was part of his charm.

He opened the car door and I got out, noting the changes since our last meeting. He was heavier. Not gross, but definitely with a tendency in that direction. Gone were the boyish good looks, replaced now by stronger features. The light brown hair, as thick as ever, was well cut. The general effect not quite handsome, but pleasing enough. However, I was amused, and not a little relieved, to discover that there was not even a glimmer of the old spark which had lit those days of my youth.

'Let's get inside,' Peter said. 'Those clouds mean business.'

Jessica opened the front door and there was a look of surprise on her face, and a hint of annoyance which seemed to be directed at Peter. I began to suspect that there might be more to this casual invitation than a simple delve into my love life.

Peter joined us for a quick coffee.

'I'm on my way to see Aunt Harriet,' he said, and from the forced enthusiasm in his voice I wondered whether he had sensed my doubts. 'I don't want to break up the party.' He glanced from Jessica to me. 'Why don't we all go? I'm sure she'd love to see you, Emma.'

'A great idea,' I said, and to my surprise Jessica looked relieved, despite the fact that an inquisition on my immediate past was now highly unlikely, and I had been so sure that it was the prime reason for the invitation. Perhaps I was misjudging her.

The rain was tippling down when we set off in Peter's car for Harriet's house in the older residential part of the town, agreeing to have a pub lunch afterwards.

'You're going to see quite a change in her,' Peter warned me as he turned in to the spacious parking-area in front of the house.

'Why do I get the feeling that you two cooked this up between you?' I said.

There was a brief and awkward silence, and then Peter said, 'Don't blame Jess. To be honest, we're out of our depth. We need another opinion.'

'On what?'

'On Aunt Harriet ... her state of mind. Has she lost her marbles or what?'

'Why ask me?'

'You've had more experience of odd situations than we have,' Jessica said.

'Oh *no!*' I said decisively, recognizing the danger signals from bitter experience. 'I've had enough "odd situations" to last me a lifetime. This is *your* problem, and you've got to deal with it.'

If I had been indifferent to Harriet's plight, I would have left there and then, but Peter had already put his thumb on the doorbell. I didn't want to upset Harriet by letting her see me depart in haste and, a sucker for punishment, I waited with them.

It seemed a long time before there was any response to the ringing of the bell. At last, the curtain covering the window at the side of the door was tweaked back, but only enough for an eye to inspect us from the slim gap. Another pause as two bolts were drawn back and the door was opened on the chain.

'Peter . . . who've you got with you?' The voice was of an old woman. I had never thought of Harriet as being old.

'We've brought Emma to see you . . . Emma Warwick.'

Fumbling fingers removed the chain, and the door opened.

'I'm sorry, my dears,' she said, 'but, being here on my own, I have to be so careful these days.'

Nothing new in that situation. Harriet had been on her own for years – ever since I'd known her. I couldn't believe the change in her. She had gone from a fine-looking woman, elegant and full of life, to a frightened creature, her usual pristine hair-do now little more than wild strands of grey, framing her pale, pinched face.

We followed her through to her favourite room overlooking the garden.

She turned to me and said, apologetically, 'I don't even feel secure in my own garden, and – just look at it – there's so much that needs to be done.' She shook her head sadly. 'What am I to do? Have they told you what's been happening here?'

Jessica led her aunt to a chair. 'Darling! You're not still worrying about that stupid man? It's not like you to get upset about something so trivial. You mustn't let it get you down like this.'

Harriet looked at me. 'If you've heard their version you probably agree with them. Do you think I'm going off my head?'

'Of course you're not going off your head,' I protested. 'And, no, Jessica and Peter haven't told me anything – except that they are worried about you.'

'If only Edward were still alive. He'd know what to do.'

Harriet had met and married Edward Travers when they were both with the Control Commission in Germany at the end of the Second World War. He was several years older than Harriet. She was already widowed when I first met her.

'What are you doing for lunch?' Peter asked her and – not waiting for a reply – added, 'Come with us to the Crown. It'll do you good to get out for a while.'

She shook her head. 'I'm in no state to go out.'

'Then, we'll get a take-away and come back here. You and Emma can have a chat while we're out of the way.' He dragged his sister towards the door. 'Come on, Jess.' And he called to me, 'You'd better close the door after us.'

I followed them, angry now, knowing I couldn't back out.

'We'll stretch it out a bit,' he said, 'Give you time to hear what she has to say. We just want to get your reaction, that's all.'

'Don't forget the chain,' Harriet called.

I slipped it into place and went back into the room to sit in the chair next to hers, looking out at the overgrown grass and the plants in need of dead-heading.

'I have no wish to burden you with my worries,' she said.

'And I don't want to pry nor, if I'm honest, do I wish to get involved in any way,' I said. 'But, Jessica and Peter are concerned about you. Sometimes it helps to talk.'

She was silent, entwining the fingers of her shaking hands, trying to keep control of her obvious distress.

I got up and looked out of the window, giving her time to calm down.

At last, she said, 'It began with a telephone call in the early hours of one morning, I suppose, four . . . five weeks ago. Maybe longer. I can't be sure. It was someone wanting to get in touch with Edward.' She sighed. 'Ten years too late.'

I returned to the chair at her side. 'An old friend?' I asked, trying to help her to organize her thoughts.

'No . . . at least . . . I don't think so. You can imagine . . . I was not exactly at my best. It was well past midnight. I don't think he gave his name.' She shook her head. 'I'm so tired. I really can't remember, but he spoke with a slight accent . . . German perhaps. You know how the phone accentuates that sort of thing.' She paused. 'But the call came from the USA.'

'He told you that?'

10

'Not directly. I was a bit short with him for ringing so late, and he said something about forgetting the five-hour difference in the clocks in New York. He wanted to know if Edward's elder brother, who had been killed in the Dunkirk evacuation, had left any photographs of mutual friends in pre-war Germany – of them, and their home. I was still at school in 1940. I suppose I was a bit vague in my reply.'

'I'm not surprised,' I said. 'I think I'd have told him to ring at a civilized hour.'

She gave a weak smile. 'He got agitated – downright rude. I hung up.'

'Have you any idea whose photographs he was after?'

'I think so. Edward often spoke of his brother, George, who had worked in Germany in the Thirties. At social gatherings, George met a variety of interesting people, on a casual basis, but he had a lot in common with a young couple who ran a flourishing antiques business. He developed an interest in antiques and began to collect in a small way, becoming a perfectionist with a good eye for the genuine article. The friendship – founded on this, and on a mutual love of music – strengthened with the years. Michael and Klara became two of his closest friends.' She glanced around the room, pointing out two pieces of furniture, and a delightful landscape in oils. I still have the furniture and the paintings and porcelain which came to Edward when George was killed.'

'Things must have changed when war broke out,' I said.

'The change came earlier than that. Although not many people knew it, Michael had Jewish blood. The time came when influential friends were no longer enough to provide a safety barrier. Michael accepted the danger of their position almost too late, but George – who some months earlier had been recalled to London and had set up house in a village near Henley-on-Thames – helped to arrange their passage to the USA.'

'That can't have been easy,' I said.

'They were accustomed to travelling all over the globe to replenish their stock, and to fulfil commissions for local dignitaries, whose influence may have kept them unmolested. But time was running out. They could take only what might be accepted as luggage for a short business trip to New York. Everything they had left behind was confiscated, including their beautiful home. They must have been heart-broken. I never saw them or their house, of course, but George had taken lots of photographs, and they were sent to Edward after George's death. I still have them.'

'And you believe that these are what the phone call was all about?'

She nodded. 'But I can't think why the wretched man got so inflamed about a collection of snaps.'

'Nostalgia perhaps,' I said.

'Oh no, it was more than that.'

'It might be worth trying to contact Michael and Klara.'

'I thought of that, but they were part of George's past, not ours. Edward only knew of them by their first names. They never met.'

'Perhaps the house still exists,' I said.

Harriet shook her head. 'At the end of the war Edward and I were both with the Military Government in Germany and, when we were stationed in Hanover for a couple of months, we drove around each weekend trying to find George's friends' old home. When we did stumble on the right location, there was nothing to see but the remains of the curving staircase and a pile of rubble. No one would admit to having known the family who had lived there, but Edward left an address where we could be contacted. It was the address of our solicitor in England.'

'So . . . someone could have had the means of tracking you down,' I said. 'But, no reputable solicitor would give a stranger your address or telephone number without first contacting you.'

'I rang him the morning after I received the phone call. He assured me that there had been no enquiries there, and that no information would have been given without my permission.'

'End of story,' I said.

'I wish I could believe that, but I'm quite sure that there's more to it than that. Someone is watching this house.'

'Unlikely to be connected with the phone call from New York,' I said, feeling that she was stretching the barriers of chance with too much vigour.

'Oh! Let's talk about something else,' she said sharply. 'I must congratulate you on the restoration of Martinsfield House.' Her voice was formal now, and I could see the difficulty she was having to disguise the annoyance my last remark had caused.

'I'm sorry, Harriet,' I said. 'I didn't mean to upset you. You must admit it's a bit of a long shot to connect one with the other.'

'But not impossible?' she insisted.

I couldn't argue with that. 'This person who is watching your house . . . someone you would recognize again?' I asked.

She looked unsure and glanced at her watch. 'He's often in the bus shelter at the other side of the road. He could be there now.'

'Couldn't simply be waiting for a bus, I suppose?' I said, unable to suppress a smile.

'If you think it's so amusing, just come upstairs. There's a bus due in a few minutes. If he is there, let's see if he takes it.'

On our way, she opened the doors of two of the bedrooms to show me more of George's treasures. I was captivated by a small lacquer cabinet in Harriet's bedroom.

'I love it too,' she said, 'but it's a fake. George got it for a song, from his German friends. Perhaps they were ashamed of being taken in. It doesn't worry me. I find it charming.'

Standing back from the bedroom window, we could see one small boy at the bus stop. There was no one in the shelter.

As we went downstairs, I said, 'You're an intelligent woman,

Harriet. Don't you think you could be seeing trouble where none exists?'

'No,' she said emphatically. 'But don't ask me for a logical explanation. Truly, I am *not* imagining things. I feel . . . threatened.'

I knew enough about gut reactions to make me wary of dismissing her fears, and yet I could not understand why Harriet was so scared. If the telephone call had come from someone with a case of chronic nostalgia, amounting perhaps to an obsession, and if he should ring again, there would be no great difficulty in having the photographs copied and sent across the Atlantic. That would be the end of it. And the snooper could be just that: one of those people who can't resist looking over fences into other people's houses; or just someone who uses the bus shelter for a breathing space on his way into the town.

'There's one thing we could do,' I said. 'I could take the photographs and have them copied. Then, if you discover that the telephone call came from someone with a perfectly genuine reason for wanting them, you can decide whether or not he can have a set. If, on the other hand, we discover that there is something devious behind this sudden interest in the past, the fact that there is another set in a safe place – at the bank, perhaps, or with your solicitor – should put you in a stronger position. It would be pointless for anyone to hassle you again.'

'Emma! I can't tell you how wonderful it is to be taken seriously for a change.' She was near to tears – not tears of self-pity, but pure relief.

I gave her a hug and said, 'It will probably turn out to be something quite innocent. The watcher in the bus shelter may be short of puff, and simply takes a rest on his way into town.'

'You're right.' She smiled. 'Was that the car? I think I've got my appetite back.'

I opened the door, and the delicious aroma rising from the

containers in the laden carrier bags made it obvious that they had been to the town's favourite Italian restaurant.

Harriet was in the kitchen putting the plates to warm. 'It's a bit chilly for the garden,' she said, handing the cutlery to me. 'We'll eat in here.'

I agreed. The kitchen, gently warmed by the heat from the Aga, had a solid-oak table in the alcove at the far end, beyond which a glazed door led out to the herb garden.

'Well, you wasted no time,' Peter said in my ear, putting the glasses and a bottle of Chianti on the table. 'I don't know what you said to her, but perhaps she'll listen to reason now.'

'I've done next to nothing – apart from listen,' I said.

'Peter!' Harriet called from the other end of the kitchen. 'Help me to load this trolley, and then we're all set.'

It was a relaxed meal. The food was good, and the tension had lifted. However, in the back of my mind I knew that we were no further down the track of finding out whether or not there had been anything to justify Harriet's earlier anxiety.

By the time we reached coffee, the sky had cleared and the sun encouraged us to go outside where the fragrance of the herb garden was breathtaking. We sat on a bench which had been sheltered from the rain by the overhanging roof of the garden shed, but an intermittent flash of light kept bothering us.

'I think it must be the boys from the property which backs on to my garden. They've recently acquired a tree house,' Harriet said. 'I haven't been in the garden very much lately, but I must have a word with them. I don't want to spoil their fun. They probably don't realize how uncomfortable it can be.'

Peter stood up to get a better look, but there was nothing to be seen. 'I'm afraid I'm going to have to break up the party,' he said, 'but I must make a move.' He glanced at his aunt. 'I have a feeling that the last sparkle of light came from further left than the tree house. It could be the sun catching a reflective surface. Don't

15

risk getting on the wrong side of your neighbours until you make sure.'

'You could be right,' she said.

'The photographs,' I reminded her. 'Can you let me have them now?'

'Of course, my dear.'

When she was out of hearing range I told Peter and Jessica what I had arranged to do.

'Quite unnecessary,' Peter said. 'It'll cost an arm and a leg. I'm fairly sure there are no negatives to work from.'

'No problem,' I said. 'It was my idea. I'll pay the bill.'

'You're wasting your time and your money. The old girl has got over the jitters. Forget it.'

Harriet's return stopped what seemed like the start of a heated argument. She handed me a large box and, with Peter champing at the bit and pointing at his watch, I took the hint and we left.

The door closed behind us and there was no mistaking the sound of the bolts being pushed home, and the chain being replaced.

Harriet was taking no chances.

Chapter 2

Picking up my car, I left Jessica and Peter congratulating themselves on getting Harriet off their consciences.

I stopped in the town to arrange for the photographs to be copied, and was somewhat shaken to discover what my involvement was going to cost. Peter had a point. No matter. If it helped Harriet to shake off the jitters, it would be worth every penny.

The man behind the counter seemed fascinated by the motley collection of prints.

'You can get a bit tired of bodies on the beach,' he said with a wry grin. 'I'll enjoy doing these.'

'When can I pick them up?'

'I can't promise them until Wednesday.' I suppose my disappointment was obvious, because he added quickly, 'Well, if I'm not pushed . . . Tuesday . . . that suit you?'

'Thank you. That'll be fine. Please don't hand them over to anyone but me. That really is important.'

'Wouldn't dream of it, Dr Warwick.'

'You know my name?'

I was surprised because I was fairly sure that I had never seen him when I'd been in the shop on previous occasions.

'Not many people around here who don't,' he said. 'You've been in our local paper several times, and in the nationals, of course. Things a bit quieter now, are they?'

'You could say that. I hope they'll stay that way.' I paused at the door. 'I think you'd better make that two sets of prints.'

'Er . . . leave it until late Tuesday morning if that's all right.'

I agreed, but it wasn't until I was back in the car that I began to accept that I was taking Harriet's worries seriously, and without any concrete evidence to support her flimsy story. Something was nagging me, something I had read in a newspaper or weekend magazine fairly recently, just skimmed through, so that it was difficult to recall with any accuracy.

I went back to the flat and recovered the stack of newspapers ready to be taken to the recycling bin in the car-park. At last, I spotted the brief account. Art treasures offered for sale had been identified as belonging to a Jewish family all but wiped out during the holocaust. Only one member of the family remained. His lengthy research had brought results. A court case was pending and was probably stirring doubts and anxiety in many quarters.

My guess was that Harriet had read this and had linked it with the telephone call and the snooper in the bus shelter.

I decided to go back over the same ground, partly because I needed a clear head to concentrate on my next assignment – and I couldn't hope for that if I had a guilty conscience about leaving Harriet in a constant state of anxiety – and partly because I was now fairly sure that the relief shown by Jessica and Peter was premature. Although Harriet had felt pleased to be listened to for a change, her reaction on our departure was to pull up the draw-bridge.

Parking the car, and with no definite plan in mind, I made for the road where the houses backed onto Harriet's garden. It was a reasonably affluent area with late Victorian houses and spacious gardens. Listing had come too late to save some of the houses on the far side of the road where a hotel, an uninspired square slab with regimented windows, occupied a corner site.

I had more or less worked out where Harriet's house fitted in, when two boys on mountain bikes whipped past me on the pavement and cut in front of me into the drive entrance of the house I had just pinpointed. I was right. Through the gap at the side of the house, where they had left the gates open, I could see down the garden to the little wooden house perched in a chestnut tree.

'I told you someone was spying on us,' one of the boys shouted to the other, and I thought he was referring to me until I saw that he was pointing to a dancing light near one corner of the tree house. 'Look! There it is again.'

'Big deal!' The second boy was not impressed. 'It's just Jimmy. He's jealous. His dad won't let him have a den like ours.'

I walked on. At least it looked as though there was nothing sinister about the annoying light. I hoped the man at the bus stop might prove equally harmless. The sun had disappeared behind black clouds, and it was beginning to rain again. A passing shower, I decided, and – on impulse – crossed the road and went into the hotel for some tea and, with a bit of luck, a sight of the visitors' book.

An elderly man was coming down the stairs as I passed the lift. He paused on the bottom step, allowing me to precede him to the reception desk. I thanked him and asked the receptionist if it was possible to have a pot of tea. She took my damp coat, indicated a table in the window and, at the same time, took the man's key.

'It's still raining quite hard, Mr Smith,' she called after him, but he brushed aside any suggestion that he should wait until it stopped.

'I must find where that bird is nesting, I need some more illustrations for my book.'

The outdoor life clearly suited him. Mr Smith was no slouch. He was a transatlantic visitor, and that was for sure. A coincidence, I told myself firmly.

The receptionist waited until he had gone and then turned to me with a broad grin on her face. 'He wants to find a robin's nest, would you believe?'

'I'd have thought there were better places for bird-watching,' I said.

'He told me his book is to be a comparison of the bird populations in various European urban areas, and this is one of them.'

She picked up the phone to order my tea. While she was looking away, I took the opportunity to have a swift glance down the page of the open visitors' book. Mr Smith came from New York.

By the time the tea arrived, the rain had almost stopped.

I asked for a brochure on my way out, and the receptionist, who was about to go off duty, offered to show me around.

I had noted the number on Mr Smith's key. Room 38. It turned out to be a corner room on the third floor, high enough to have a wide view of the surrounding gardens. I was shown an adjoining room, and was surprised to see how good the view was. There was plenty of space between the houses. Perhaps not such a bad spot for bird-watching after all.

'I suppose, as an architectural historian, you don't approve of the hotel being here?' the receptionist said.

It seemed I couldn't avoid being recognized.

'Not entirely,' I admitted.

'Locally, they call it the "Warehouse",' she said.

I smiled. 'The description is not entirely undeserved.'

'It's become almost a term of endearment,' she said. 'The manager says that after the initial shock, the locals found it a useful meeting place, and our guests return time after time.'

'From the USA too, if I'm not mistaken.'

'Oh . . . Mr Smith,' she said. 'This is his first visit, and he obviously came here with one aim in mind – to complete another chapter of his book. I don't suppose we'll see him again. Just a one-off. He's a bit of a loner. When he's not out taking photographs, he's up in his room in a comfortable armchair in front of the open window, with some pretty powerful field-glasses. We've had one or two complaints from local residents, but now that they know what he's up to, and that their gardens may have a slot in his next book, they're beginning to regard him as part of the landscape.'

We walked out of the hotel together.

'I wouldn't mind betting I know where our Mr Smith is now,' she said.

'Show me,' I challenged her.

We crossed the road, took the first turning on the left, then left again into the road where Harriet lived. We had walked only a short distance from the corner when she nudged me, but I had already seen him in the bus shelter, field-glasses focused in Harriet's direction.

'Full marks,' I said as we turned to retrace our footsteps. 'I must go and pick up my car. Can I give you a lift?'

I was glad that she refused, because I wanted to get back to Harriet, but not on foot. I wanted to be in my car, where I might not be recognized by the persistent ornithologist.

It was only a short walk to the car-park and, when I turned into the drive about five minutes later, Mr Smith was no longer in sight.

'Harriet!' I called through the letter box, getting no reply from my efforts with the doorbell. 'It's Emma. *Please* let me in.'

I was almost beginning to give up hope when I heard the bolts being drawn and the key being turned in the lock. The door opened a crack, and I got a glimpse of Harriet's anxious face.

The chain was released.

I went inside, and the whole procedure was reversed until Harriet felt secure again.

'The man across the road. I know who he is,' I said, and told her about seeing the boys, and their den in the branches, and went on to describe my visit to the hotel and my brief contact with the man who was writing a book about the birds in European urban areas, the man whose search for a robin's nest in the trees had almost certainly generated the annoying flashes of light when, from the open window of his room on the third floor, the sunlight had been reflected from the lenses of his field-glasses.

'Ornithologist! And you believe that?' she said cynically.

'Open mind. It's just crazy enough to be true.'

'An ornithologist would know better than to look for a robin's nest in the trees. He would be scouring the hedgerows.'

'Well . . . American robins are different, aren't they?' I said, grabbing at straws.

'So? My dear Emma, he's supposed to be writing a book. Even a hack would have researched the basic facts.'

I wanted to convince Harriet, and myself, that Mr Smith was simply a lonely old man who might, or might not, be writing a book on urban birds. His roost in the bus shelter was probably entirely innocent. Perhaps this solitary creature needed some excuse to wander the world on his own.

Selfishly, I was getting desperate for an escape from this tangle. At first encounter, it had seemed possible that I could put Harriet's mind at rest by proving that there was nothing to worry about. But I had to convince myself too. There were too many things that didn't quite add up.

'Makes you think, doesn't it?' Harriet said quietly, noting my indecision.

I nodded, but said nothing for a while. I was trying to make sense of the facts as I knew them, and to fit them together.

At last, I said, 'Let me present you with a hypothesis.'

'Fire away,' she said crisply, and I followed her into the kitchen where the kettle was grumbling gently on the Aga.

This was more like the Harriet I knew. I could feel the change in her attitude: she was suddenly more confident. Her back had straightened. I began to hope that we were winning.

'Before I air my ideas, you do realize that you have some very valuable possessions?' I said, with some diffidence.

'Yes, of course. And you haven't seen them all – not by a long way. Everything was left to Edward when George was killed. Edward was in the Army by then. He sold the house. I believe the basic furniture and fittings were part of the sale, and the personal and more valuable contents were put into storage in the country. This, of course, was before I had met Edward. I was still at school.'

'But the items could now be identified as your property?'

She nodded. 'I have all the documentation. Edward's will, of course. His brother's too, and the provenance of each and every item, including the photographs which you took to be copied.'

'You need copies of the documents too,' I said. 'I have a photo-copier in the flat and, if you can give them to me now, I'll let you have them back tomorrow, with the copies. Your solicitor should have the originals. They'll be safer with him. We'll get them to him on Monday morning.'

'You make it all seem so straightforward.'

'I'm looking at it from the outside,' I said. 'That simplifies matters.'

'Perhaps ... but I can't tell you how much your help and support means to me,' Harriet said. 'And now I'm getting us side-tracked again, and I do so want to hear your views.'

It was difficult to hold on to a feasible theory. So much of the story had vanished into history.

'When you and Edward were in Germany at the end of the Second World War and went searching for the house of Michael and Klara, do you think it possible that you might have spoken to someone – more than one, perhaps – who knew where the contents of the house had been taken?'

She shrugged her shoulders. 'They might have had them in

their own cellars for all we knew. It was a delicate situation. Our transfer to the Hanover area was only a temporary assignment. We had no authority to make any enquiries.' She paused. 'There could have been one or two people on the snaps we took at the time. If so, they'll be with that batch I gave you earlier.'

'We get those back on Tuesday,' I said. 'But, taken over fifty years ago . . . I don't suppose they're going to tell us anything vital now. But, consider this: could there have been someone out there when you visited the site, possibly an ex-employee of Michael and Klara, who might have got wind of what was going on in those months before war broke out, and had taken the pick of the furniture and pictures – items which were still in the house, as well as those stored on the commercial premises – before the remainder was confiscated?'

'Help would have been needed to get things safely out of the way before the authorities realized that Michael and Klara were not coming back,' Harriet said. 'There would have been porcelain and silver too . . . so many *objets d'art.*'

'Once in a safe hiding place, nothing could be moved until all risk of discovery could be ignored,' I went on. 'Then the war came, and nothing could be done until it was long over and it became worth the risk of chancing a sale – perhaps a small piece of furniture sent with other items to London, Paris, or New York. Testing the market. Or a painting, or porcelain, offered to a private collector . . . no questions asked?'

'One sale? A solitary item?' Harriet asked.

'More than one item, and someone might have made a connection. Remember, we are talking of the top of the market.'

'But why should someone try to contact Edward now? If you're even remotely on target,' Harriet said, 'why risk drawing attention to something which could have continued as before? And why the interest in the old photographs? It seems to me they could only make that person more vulnerable.'

'Possibly . . . if the evidence remains intact.' I paused, wanting to make my point, but also wanting Harriet to realize that I was not shrugging off her fears. 'Things have changed recently, provenance is all-important. The original conspirators if they exist now – if they ever existed – are old. If my guess is anywhere near the truth, they have kept their greed under control, doubtless doing well enough on the proceeds over the years. But, now that things are changing, they'll be wanting to close the book before it snaps shut, trapping their sticky fingers . . . or before they are no longer around to benefit.'

Harriet nodded her head, but was looking at me as though I had said something indelicate. There was a faint smile on her lips.

'Damn it! Harriet. I'm not lumping you in with him . . . them . . . whatever. You must have been in your early twenties when you were in Germany. When would it be? 1946?'

She nodded. 'Late '46. I was twenty-one.'

'So? Supposing this theory is anywhere near the truth, that would make it at least seven years on from the original theft. They would probably be in or near their thirties at the end of the war.' I paused. 'Harriet . . . I know this is simply supposition, and we'll probably laugh ourselves silly when we find out the truth, but we can't ignore that it *could* be possible that someone is interested in the contents of this house, or fears that you may have proof of original ownership of the items which belonged to George's old friends.'

There was an embarrassed silence between the two of us, and then Harriet said, 'Or is it simply that I have blown it up out of all proportion? And, perhaps, we have both been reading too much in the newspapers on this subject?'

'Maybe. But, I've come to respect the concept of "safety first", and I still don't like to think of you being on your own. I have a dinner date tonight, otherwise I'd suggest that you come back home with me right now.'

'I couldn't leave the house.' She was digging in her heels, and I could see the tension building up again.

'We're no further forward, are we?' I said.

'I don't feel so isolated now. But, in the background, there's still that feeling of . . . menace.'

'Stay with Jessica or Peter tonight, or – if you don't want to leave the house – ask one of them to stay with you. And let the police know about Mr Smith's activities.'

'They'll think I'm an idiot,' she protested. 'If he's some sort of villain, he would hardly advertise his presence.'

'And if it's some form of intimidation, I'd say it has worked. How long is it since you went outside your front door?'

'A month . . . six weeks . . .' Her face was a blank. 'I don't know. I can't remember. Oh, Emma! It seems like . . . forever. What a *fool* I've been. I'm so ashamed. You should never have been dragged into this.'

'It can't be dismissed until we know what it's all about,' I said. 'There's too much that needs explaining. Just have a word with the police – promise me. I'll feel easier in my mind.'

'Well . . . if you insist.'

'And Jessica and Peter . . .'

'Don't bully me. I've got the message. I'll speak to Jessica first. At least Barry won't be around.' She checked herself.

'You don't like him?' I said, and I couldn't help grinning when I saw the relief on her face as she realized that I too found him a bit of a pain.

'Not what you'd call . . . enthusiastic,' she said, the flicker of a smile playing on her lips, and then she continued as though the slight hiccup had not occurred. 'If Jessica can't come here, I'll have a word with Peter.'

'I'll ring you in the morning,' I said, wishing I could contact Maxwell and cancel our meeting, for it was he who was taking me out to dinner. He was at a meeting in London and his mobile phone would be switched off – its normal mode. Maxwell uses a mobile in emergencies, or when he has arranged to be contacted, otherwise he prefers to be out of reach.

Chapter 3

Back at the flat, and waiting for Maxwell to arrive, I thought I'd give Harriet a ring to make sure she was all right. I was about to try once more when an incoming call took me by surprise.

'What the hell d'you think you're doing, Emma?' It was Peter, ready to explode by the sound of it.

'I'm about to go out to dinner,' I said, as blandly as I could manage, a bit thrown by the hostility of his approach.

'You know what I mean. Aunt Harriet wants me to go round there tonight. To sleep! And I thought you'd got her to see a bit of sense at last. Why in heaven's name did you want to go back again this afternoon and spoil everything?'

'You didn't want me to make her see sense,' I said. 'You wanted me to get her out of your hair, or off your conscience . . . and, so help me, I don't know which I despise more.'

There was silence at the other end of the line.

'Nothing to say?' I wanted to make him squirm.

'Oh, plenty,' he said acidly. 'Jess and I think it could be time for her to go into some sort of home.'

'You're not serious?'

'You bet I'm serious. We can't go on like this.'

'What's getting at you, Peter? It surely wouldn't hurt you, or Jessica, to spend one night making Harriet feel reasonably secure

. . . or are you too wrapped up in yourselves even to manage that?'

'Has it ever struck you that there are times when you can be a real bitch?'

That knocked me back a little.

'I speak my mind, if that's what you mean,' I said. 'Can't we just get back to the problem in hand?'

'And what's that, exactly?'

'You know perfectly well. Harriet feels threatened. That's the way she put it to me, and I must admit I agree that there *could* be logical grounds for her fears. All right . . . improbable . . . but impossible to ignore.'

'Well, you can forget about Aunt Harriet now. If the antique furniture and other valuables are not in the house, she'll feel safer. We'll get it all sorted out. The valuables are willed to us anyway. You can get on with your new project and earn yourself some more publicity, but not at the expense of an ageing woman. We'll take care of Aunt Harriet.'

I opened my mouth to protest, but Peter was no longer at the other end.

I was too shaken to take it all in. Clearly, I had misinterpreted that call for help from Peter and Jessica. It seemed I was taken to see Harriet simply to rubber-stamp their plan to persuade her to give up her home. It was getting near the time when it might be sensible for her to have a little more help in the house and garden, but she was not ready to be written off. Far from it.

I hesitated before dialling Jessica's number, but I needed to confirm that she and Peter were looking at things from the same viewpoint.

'Hello . . .' The voice at the other end was a little uncertain.

'Jessica, what are you and Peter up to?'

'I don't know what you mean.'

The plea of injured innocence made me cringe. 'Give me

credit for a bit of common sense,' I snapped. 'You dragged me in simply to support your aim to get Harriet out of her home. Why?'

'It's none of your business.'

'You made it my business.'

'Well, I'm sorry if that's what you think.' She sounded not at all sorry. 'I was a fool to get you involved. Just forget it.'

'It's not quite as simple as that,' I said. 'There's something wrong somewhere.'

'These days, you think everyone's a crook. Really, Emma . . . you're getting pathetic.'

'If you're right, then I apologize,' I said. 'But, I still believe there could be something odd going on. Seeing that man at the hotel . . . a bit eccentric . . . made me wonder, that's all.'

'What man? At which hotel?'

'Of course, I haven't seen you since we left Harriet after lunch,' I said, and told her then of my visit to the photographer, and of my decision to nose around the area. I told her of the probable reason for the light which had worried Harriet, and of my brief contact with the American ornithologist, including seeing him standing in the bus shelter.

There was a prolonged silence.

'Jessica . . . Jessica!' I said. 'Are you there?'

Still no reply. I was about to replace the receiver when I heard her say, 'Leave it, Emma. Just . . . leave it.'

If she had wanted to make me continue with my probing which I doubted – she could not have chosen a better method.

It took me a moment to realize that the entry bell for my flat was ringing.

'Is that you, Maxwell?'

'Who else?' the gruff voice said, and I pressed the button to allow him in, and waited for the lift doors to open.

'You look ravishing, as usual,' he said, planting a casual kiss on the end of my nose.

'Oh, Maxwell . . . it is good to see you.'

He stood back and eyed me with some disquiet.

'Good? Then why am I receiving distress signals?'

'I can't imagine,' I said lightly.

'You can't fool me, and we're not budging from here until you tell me what's wrong.'

'Later,' I insisted. 'I've been looking forward to this evening. Let's not spoil it. It's probably something that will solve itself anyway. And . . . you'll hate this . . . I think I may be getting the reputation for seeking publicity.'

'You deserve recognition for the work you do.'

'I don't object to that, but it's the sensational stuff which most people seem to remember.'

Peter's jibe had bitten deeper than I had realized.

Maxwell took me to an old country inn with high-backed settles. The whole atmosphere was relaxing, and the food and wine couldn't be faulted, but my mind kept returning to Harriet.

When the coffee was poured, Maxwell leant across the table and, putting a hand over mine, said, 'Don't you think it's time to tell me what's going on?'

I didn't want to spoil the evening, but I did need his view of that day's events. Starting with that morning's meeting with Jessica, I gave him the whole sequence, concentrating on the facts, trying to keep clear of my own reactions.

When I had finished, Maxwell remained silent.

I waited impatiently for his verdict, trying not to break his concentration, until at last I said, 'You think I'm making too much of it, don't you?'

'It's possible that there are simple explanations for what's been going on,' he said, and I thought he was going to shrug it off as over-active imagination on my part, coupled with the quirky mind of an elderly woman. However, he continued: 'But, like you, my dear Emma, I believe I can smell trouble.'

The comfort of being taken seriously made me realize just how much Harriet had suffered.

'It really has got to you, hasn't it?' Maxwell said.

I nodded. 'I felt there was something wrong, but it all seemed so bizarre. I needed an opinion I could trust.'

'You realize there may be nothing to it? Simply an eccentric ornithologist, and a nephew and niece who are letting their cupidity show.'

'But, you believe there's more to it than that, don't you?' I said.

'I'm not committing myself at this stage. But it is perhaps providential that I'm meeting Abbot tomorrow at the golf club.'

'Not Detective Superintendent Abbot?'

'The same.'

I was surprised. This was the senior detective involved in clearing up the trouble at Martinsfield.

'I didn't know you played golf,' I said. 'And I certainly didn't know that you were seeing Henry Abbot socially.'

'You'd be surprised at the number of things you don't know about me,' he said. 'Abbot and I play the odd round of golf. He's good company when he's not on duty.'

'You're not intending to discuss Harriet's problems?'

'Not directly,' he said. 'Troubles in the antiques market have been aired in the press several times in recent months. It could come up casually in the general conversation.' He paused. 'Why don't you bring her down to Martinsfield for a few days?'

'And leave a clear field for the interested parties . . . not likely!'

'You have a point there. Right on target. That's the Emma I know and love,' he said, smiling broadly. 'And now I'm going to take you back to your flat.' There was a lengthy pause. 'I was intending that our evening should evolve around quite a different matter.'

He didn't attempt to elaborate until we were back in the apartment, but then he wasted no time.

'I've been thinking seriously about Martinsfield, and I'd like it to have a useful function – something that will in no way impair what has already been achieved.'

'You have something definite in mind?' I said, relieved that he did not appear to want a change in our easy relationship.

'Yes, but it would need your collaboration.'

'Tell me more.'

He paused, as though unsure where to begin, and then he said, 'When you took on the Martinsfield project you knew where to find the right craftsmen.'

'I was lucky enough to have worked with two firms who had very good reputations,' I said. 'I knew their work, and that they took pride in it. And they knew where to find other craftsmen for the work they don't normally cover. It was a great team.'

'Exactly. But what if we could develop a centre with well-equipped workshops, manned by men and women who could take on similar problems to the ones we encountered in the resurrection of Martinsfield, and who could also pass on their specialized knowledge?'

'You're serious, aren't you?' I said. 'Do you realize what you'd be taking on?'

'On my own – it would be impossible. But with a resident architectural historian to get it off the ground . . .'

'Hold on!' I cut in, ignoring the "resident" bit for the moment. 'There'd be planning permission . . . no end of red tape to cope with.'

'I've put out feelers already.'

'Any particular reason for wanting to do this?' I asked.

'It seemed like a gap worth filling. And . . .'

'And?'

'You'd be around the place more often.' The twisted smile

showed a touch of embarrassment – something alien to his nature. 'I miss you, Emma.'

In the few short weeks I'd been back at the flat, I'd missed him too, but I didn't think it was the right moment to admit it. We'd kept our relationship low-key, and that was how I wanted it to remain.

I spent a sleepless night, with Maxwell's scheme for the future of Martinsfield teasing me into enthusiasm, making me eager to see it in action. The difficulties of such a venture could not be ignored. They began to surface, one after the other, building up like a nightmare – although I was still wide awake.

I was on the point of dismissing the whole concept as a pipe-dream when I remembered being told how the stunning restoration of Uppark in West Sussex had revealed a cache of hidden talent just waiting to be encouraged and developed. I went to sleep with enthusiasm spilling over, and woke up to a dreary Sunday morning: grey sky and drenching rain.

I had half hoped that Jessica might ring and confirm that she, or Peter, had stayed the night at Harriet's place, but I should have known better. I spent part of the morning photocopying the documents Harriet had handed over the previous afternoon, and I waited until 11.30 before tapping out Jessica's number.

'Hello, Jessica,' I said, when at last she lifted the receiver. 'Just ringing to find out how Harriet is this morning. Did you sleep there? Or, is she with you?' I felt fairly certain that Peter would have steered clear.

'No to both questions,' she said coolly. 'And I am not intending to see Aunt Harriet today. If she won't take our advice, then she can't expect us to come running every time there's someone in the bus shelter.'

It was I who put the phone down this time.

There was no reply from Harriet's number, so I put the morning's work in large envelopes, and the originals in my briefcase. Five minutes later, with an armful of precious documents, I was standing at Harriet's front door, ringing the bell. I could hear the shrill tone, but there was no sound of movement, no twitching of the curtain in the window beside the door. She could still be in bed, but I thought it unlikely.

I waited a minute or two more. Then, after returning the envelopes and briefcase to the boot, and double-checking that I had locked it, I walked around to the back of the house. The door to the kitchen was ajar. With some trepidation I went inside, and my heart turned over as I saw Harriet lying in a crumpled heap beside the door into the hall.

She must have been there for some time. Her head was caked with dried blood, and one arm was outstretched as though to reach the phone on the work surface above her. I called her name, but there was no response. Dragging the phone down beside me, I got through to the emergency services, at the same time feeling Harriet's wrist and, to my great relief, finding a weak pulse.

Ambulance and police were on their way. I was afraid to move her, knowing that I might do more harm than good, also that the police would not welcome anything that might cover up what had happened.

It was less than five minutes later – although it seemed much longer – when the doorbell rang and running feet came to the back of the house and in at the kitchen door. A young policeman went through to the front door and opened up. The ambulance had arrived almost at the same time.

I got to my feet and stood back out of the way. The sooner Harriet got to hospital the better. A low whimper as she was lifted on to the stretcher was the only indication of life, but a welcome one.

I stepped forward and said, 'You'll be all right now, Harriet. Hang on.'

She showed no sign of having heard and, with the sergeant at my elbow, I watched her go with a policewoman assigned to accompany her.

'And you are. . . ?' the sergeant said, turning back to me.

'Dr Emma Warwick.'

His eyebrows lifted. 'Well, well! Trouble follows you around, doesn't it?'

I made no comment, and he said, looking at his notes, 'And the lady who has just made her exit, is. . . ?'

'Mrs Harriet Travers.'

'Are you her next of kin?'

'No,' I said, and gave him addresses and telephone numbers for Jessica and Peter.

'Sarge!' The call came from a constable standing in the doorway to the hall. 'It looks as though some of the furniture may have gone. Drag marks on the carpet, and some bits and pieces on the floor.'

The sergeant turned to me. 'You'd know if anything had been taken?'

'Not in accurate detail, but Mrs Travers showed me part of the house yesterday.'

'For any particular reason?'

'She didn't ring you late yesterday afternoon?'

He looked puzzled. 'We'll talk about this down at the station. First, we'll check the rooms. If we're going to make an arrest, and if anything is going to be recovered, there's no time to waste.'

'The garden room first?' I said, leading the way.

The blanks on the walls where the two small pieces of furniture had stood confirmed my fears. The oil paintings had gone too.

'Can you describe them?' he said.

'I can do better than that. Mrs Travers has the provenance of every piece she owns. Every piece of furniture, every painting, the porcelain . . . the lot.'

'Not any longer, by the look of it,' he said, calling me into the small room used as a study. 'The locks of the desk drawers have been forced. They knew what they were after.'

'But, Harriet gave it all to me, yesterday.'

'Why to you?'

I gave him a swift outline, from the original telephone call, which Harriet had received from the USA, to my efforts of the previous day.

'She agreed that I should take the photographs to be copied,' I said. 'I took them to the photographer near the corner of the High Street and School Lane. Later, when I saw her again, Mrs Travers handed over all the documentation. I photocopied the lot this morning, and we were going to take the originals to her solicitor tomorrow. I figured that with more than one copy of each of the photographs, and if the solicitor had the original documents, there would be no point in some stranger pestering Harriet.'

'The DI will want to hear about this. We'll finish our recce and get back to the station.'

In the dining-room, the Georgian sideboard and the dining table had not been removed, neither had the two wine-coolers, but the walls were denuded of paintings. In the drawing-room, Chinese porcelain and the delicate water-colours had gone. We went upstairs, but nothing seemed to have been touched up there.

'Probably thought they'd killed the old lady and were making their getaway with time on their side. I must say I'm surprised they sank to violence. Maybe not so professional after all.'

'Now that you have an idea of what has gone,' I said, 'I'd like to go straight to the hospital. Mrs Hammond and Mr Jackson know more than I do about the house contents. They'll be more use to you than I can hope to be, and I do want to find out how Harriet is.'

'Mrs Travers will be in intensive care, and I'm sure the DI will see that you are kept informed about her progress. We'll go in your car, if you've no objection.'

Chapter 4

My session with Detective Inspector Ian Foster was taking longer than I had expected. His manner was pleasant, and he was clearly an expert at getting the information he needed: innocent-sounding questions, stirring a swift response. He was a good-looking man, mid- to late-thirties. Tanned. An outdoor type.

All the documents were swiftly checked, and those relating to the missing items immediately transmitted through the network. However, this did not prevent my movements in the previous twenty-four hours being double-checked, as was my brief contact with Mr Smith. Perhaps he too had received coffee and sandwiches in lieu of Sunday lunch.

DI Foster delved into every angle – relevant or not – of my acquaintance with Harriet and her relatives, and now he was querying my knowledge of her financial situation – to which I had never given even a passing thought.

'Adequate, I suppose,' I said lamely.

'Would she keep large amounts of money in the house?'

'I've no idea, but I think it unlikely.'

'Was she in the habit of adding to her collection . . . contacting dealers, or going to sales?'

'I doubt it. Her nephew and niece would certainly be far more likely to provide an accurate answer.'

'Are you a collector of antiques, Dr Warwick?'

It was no casual enquiry. The shrewd grey eyes seemed capable of reading my mind.

'I can't afford such luxuries.'

'But you've studied the subject?'

'What gives you that idea?'

'Your occupation.'

'I'm an architectural historian, not an art historian. My studies were concentrated on architecture, and that's where my first interest lies. But, you're right, the fine arts were not neglected. Like many people, I came to appreciate beautiful things, but . . . not to covet them. I inherited a few small items from my parents, but nothing in the same league as those owned by Mrs Travers.'

I glanced at my watch.

'I won't keep you much longer, Dr Warwick,' he said, 'but I think you'll agree that Mrs Travers would want us to do everything possible to retrieve her property.' He picked up the phone and asked, 'Is there anything new from the hospital?'

I held my breath.

'Keep me informed,' he said, and swivelled his chair towards me. 'Mrs Travers has regained consciousness, but she's rather confused.'

'But . . . she'll be all right now?'

The spread hands were non-committal. 'You won't be able to see her, I'm afraid. She's in intensive care, and there are to be no visitors until we have a clearer picture of what's been going on.'

'I think she'll want to see me.'

'But not yet,' he insisted. 'She's lucky to be alive, and she has you to thank for that. Apart from the medical angle, the visiting ban is for her own safety. If we let one in, we open the floodgates. We can't risk that. She's being well looked after.'

The phone was ringing again and, answering it, he gave an impatient grunt. The partly muffled curse as he got to his feet told me that it was not good news.

'It looks as though we could be out of luck,' he said. 'The photographer had a break-in during the night.'

My hopes were shattered. It would be more difficult now to make an immediate and irrefutable identification of the items which were probably already well concealed, or even on their way to another country. But, at least it was not bad news about Harriet.

'He lives over the shop,' he went on, 'but there's no sign of him. We'd better get over there. The whole place has been ransacked. His assistant says that earlier in the week he did talk of going away for the weekend. If he's left his address with the keyholder we should be able to contact him without much delay.'

Hurrying out to the waiting car, I was still clutching my brief-case.

'I don't think the man I saw was the owner,' I said, as the driver steered into a gap in a long string of cars. 'I've been in there many times over the years. It was always a Mr . . .' I paused, trying to remember his name. 'It began with a C.'

'Carter,' DI Foster prompted.

'Yes, that's right. But that wasn't the man who was going to copy the photographs.'

'Same name – different man. Cecil Carter died about a year ago. He left the business to his brother, James.'

'You mean, he'd only been involved with the business for a year?' I said, horrified that I had handed over the photographs to someone with no real experience. 'I should have my stupid head examined! I was so convinced that he knew exactly how to deal with the faded prints.'

'Calm down, Dr Warwick. James Carter is recognized as an expert when it comes to dealing with old photographic prints. He always was a keen photographer, but the business was originally left to his elder brother. James had a good job – something to do with computers, I believe. He was happy enough to accept the status quo. The two brothers were the greatest of friends, and James was called in whenever something out of the ordinary cropped up . . . more so, after his wife died and he retired. It helped him to fill the gaps in his life. He was devastated by his brother's death, but – it has to be admitted – he was truly in his element when the business dropped into his lap. He'd been look-ing for a smaller house for some time, and decided to move into the flat above the shop.'

We were almost there. There was no sign of any break-in. The car passed the front entrance, turning left to a wide alleyway which was used for deliveries to the short row of shops. The police were keeping a low profile. Their presence could not be seen from the street.

'Any contact with Carter?' the Inspector asked the sergeant who met him at the back door.

'Not with the man himself. He was staying with his son last night, up in London. Left soon after lunch, should be here soon.'

'The sooner the better. God! What a shambles! Have you come across any photos of antiques?'

'Not one,' the sergeant said. 'Reckon they've taken the lot.'

A slight commotion behind us announced the arrival of Mr James Carter.

'Dr Warwick!' he said, storming into the room. 'What are you doing here?' Then he caught sight of Detective Inspector Foster and, pushing past me, took in the chaos of the scene. 'Ian! What the hell. . . ?'

'Sorry, James. I'm afraid your place has been taken apart.'

'I rather gathered that.'

Puzzled, he went into the small room at the back of the shop.

'Well, it doesn't look as though they were after money,' he said. 'The safe is still intact.'

'It seems they were after those photographs I left with you yesterday,' I said. 'I'm so sorry. I can't think how they knew I had them in the first place, or where I had taken them. Believe me, I would never knowingly have landed you in this mess. And all for nothing, apparently.'

'Well, the loss of the photographs needn't worry you any more,' he said, with a wry smile. 'My son and I have been working on them. Not all finished yet, I'm afraid. I'll fetch them from the car.'

It was as though the sun had just come out.

He came back carrying the large box which Harriet had handed over the previous afternoon, and he put it on his desk in the back room.

Harriet had sorted the prints relating to her own property into separate folders and, fortunately, Mr Carter had kept to the same system. But I was only given time to select the prints showing the missing items before the box was whisked away by DI Foster.

For the first time, I felt completely justified in my support of Harriet. I desperately wanted to tell her that she had been right all along. This lively attention to what could have been seen as mindless vandalism showed that it was being taken seriously.

'I suppose I'd better not ask what this is all about,' Mr Carter said with a deep sigh. The immediate rush of adrenalin was no longer effective, and he was faced with the daunting task of salvaging and identifying what was left, before his clients heard the news and came clamouring at his door. 'I can see now why you asked me not to hand over the finished product to anyone but yourself.'

'I thought I was being over-fussy,' I said. 'But they were not my photographs and I didn't want to take any chances with them.'

'I'm not blaming you, Dr Warwick. It doesn't take a genius to see that, if the prints are significant in any way, and there doesn't seem much room for doubt about that, then you could be on the edge of something extremely dodgy. This was not just a night out for the town's tearaways. I think, if I were you, I'd go fast in the opposite direction. Leave this one to the professionals.'

'I can't simply walk out on a friend,' I said.

'He, or she, wouldn't want you to take unnecessary risks,' Mr Carter said, and seeing me hesitate, he added, 'All right . . . I'm not trying to squeeze any information out of you. I'm concerned for your safety.'

So, perhaps, was DI Foster. He had sent his driver to take me back to the police station.

'The DI wants to see you before you go, ma'am,' the driver said when he drew up outside the station entrance.

I had to wait some time before the Detective Inspector was free. There was an atmosphere of urgency and excitement. I was anxious to know whether my probing into Harriet's past, combined with the feeling that there was some connection between this and the phone call from New York, had any validity; or was it simply the mental gymnastics of a suspicious mind?

'Dr Warwick, I do apologize for keeping you waiting.' He took me to his office. 'From what you told me earlier, I think you know, with a certain degree of accuracy, what this is all about.'

During his questioning that morning I had given him an outline of the hypothesis I had presented to Harriet, quite prepared for it to be shot to pieces.

'Poor Harriet,' I said. 'Nobody would take her seriously.'

'You did.'

'After some doubts. It all seemed . . . so unlikely. I thought we had been influenced by articles we'd seen in the newspapers. And yet, like Harriet, I had an uncomfortable feeling that there was something odd going on.'

'I'd have thought the obvious move would have been to inform the police.'

'Give me a chance! I only became involved yesterday . . . and I thought I had persuaded Harriet to do just that, but she can hardly be blamed for her reluctance to risk being thought a foolish old woman. She'd had enough of that already.'

44

'You didn't waste any time in doing a little investigation on your own.'

'Just checking one or two things. I take it you've already questioned Mr Smith?'

He nodded.

'It would appear that Smith *is* an ornithologist,' he said, 'but I doubt that he'll be publishing another book. His son rang us from Waterloo station. He's in London on a business trip. Gave us the number of his hotel. Told us not to rely too much on what the old man says as his father's memory is patchy.' He grinned. 'We'd already found that out for ourselves.'

'What now?' I said.

'You still live locally?'

'Yes.'

'Is there anywhere you can go until we've cleared this up?'

'I'm not running away,' I said indignantly. 'I've got a new project on the go.'

'It would be wise to get out of the way for a while,' he said. 'And to . . . be a bit more cautious than usual.'

The phone rang. When he put it down again, he got up from his desk and walked across the room. He seemed lost for words.

'It's not bad news . . . not Harriet?' I said.

'Not Mrs Travers. Your flat. There's been a fire. Leave your briefcase. It'll be quite safe here. Give me your ignition key. I'll leave it at the desk in case your car needs to be moved in an emergency.'

Chapter 5

The fire, under control by the time we got there, was confined to my flat, but the whole apartment block was affected. The smell of burning was everywhere, and the general feeling amongst the residents was that it was my fault, that I had been careless in some way. This upset me more than a little. We had always been on such good terms.

The fire chief put my mind at rest – on that score, at least.

'Definitely not your fault,' he said, as we stood on the threshold. 'Someone's got it in for you. No doubt about that.'

I turned away, sickened. The security system had never let us down before, and I began to wonder which of my accusers had pressed the button to allow a stranger into the building.

DI Foster joined us.

The police were one step ahead. They had questioned all the residents, and had pin-pointed Miss Tucker, an elderly newcomer, a real sweetie and as soft-hearted as they come, who had let in a young man when she returned from her customary afternoon walk. She had described him as well-dressed, and with charming manners. Added to that, he was carrying a large bunch of flowers, supposedly for his aunt. How could he lose?

My eyes were smarting, and the smoke was making me cough. I was not going to be allowed even to begin to clear the debris until as much information as possible had been extracted from what was left.

The original spot I had chosen for the documents relating to Harriet's valuables was in the filing cabinet which had also contained all the research notes and plans for my next project. The lock had been forced, papers were strewn everywhere, charred, and reduced to a pulp after the efforts of the firemen in containing the blaze.

Although I blessed the impulse that had made me remove Harriet's documents and the copies I had made, I had to accept that with my own papers on the new project destroyed, I would have to re-establish all the contacts, refresh my mind on all the research, and take all the measurements again. My computer, which had held every detail including interior plans, was clearly a write-off, and the back-up discs – every single one I possessed – had been added to the inferno. Hard copy, hard disc, back-up discs . . . nothing remained.

Forced to stay on the outside, looking in, I was devastated.

'Come on. Let's get you out of here,' DI Foster said, obviously accustomed to seeing people on the verge of a breakdown.

The fire chief was with his men, and I turned back to thank them for avoiding a complete disaster. No one had been injured.

'All in a day's work,' the chief said, 'but I'd watch my back, if I were you.' And looking over my shoulder, he added, 'Don't you agree, Ian?'

'I've already done my best to make that clear. Perhaps, with your endorsement, Dr Warwick will take me seriously.' He turned to me. 'Back to the station,' he said. 'With all the information we have, the stolen antiques will be impossible to move on the open market. I'm sorry about your flat but, thanks to your foresight, Mrs Travers has a better chance of getting her property back again.'

My home might be devastated, and my hard work nullified, but at least on one front we were achieving a little progress.

Back at the police station, the young constable at the front desk, flushed with excitement, said, 'They're putting road-blocks on the exits from the motorway, and the receptionist at the hotel left a message that Mr Smith has booked out – going to a quieter hotel. Oh yes, and Dr Warwick's car was collected by the mechanic.'

'What mechanic?' the DI demanded fiercely.

A look of total disaster crossed the young man's face.

'He had a note . . . on headed paper . . . signed by Dr Warwick.'

He picked up a sheet of headed paper which I recognized at once as my own; the writing was definitely not.

'Constable!' The DI looked to be close to boiling point. 'Take your fingers off that piece of paper! I want it tested for prints. And get Smith's new address. I want it on my desk in two minutes.' He turned to me. 'Unless I'm very much mistaken, your car has already had the same treatment as your flat,' he said apologetically. 'Come through to my office.'

I turned back to the poor lad at the desk. 'It's not the end of the world,' I said.

'I'm sorry, ma'am. The ignition key was here, but I should have waited until I'd checked with the duty sergeant.'

I shrugged my shoulders. 'You win some . . . you lose some. It's been that sort of a day.'

'This way, Dr Warwick.' The DI was getting impatient.

He was opening his office door when a shrill voice echoed down the corridor: 'Peter . . . you idiot! I told you she was here.' No mistaking Jessica's voice when she was in a tiz.

I was propelled into the room, and the door was firmly closed.

'I'm sure you don't relish a confrontation with Mrs Hammond right now, but I need to have a word with her, and with Mr Jackson. The main investigation is out of my hands, but we can't afford to miss even the most flimsy lead. Just bear with me for a few minutes. Susan will bring you a cup of tea.'

Illogical, on my part, it certainly was, but I was relieved to see that my briefcase was where I had left it, under my chair.

WPC Susan Crosby came in a few minutes later with a cup of tea and two biscuits.

'Wow! What a day!' she said, the adrenalin flowing like Noah's flood. 'I've only just come back from the hospital. I've been sitting with Mrs Travers since she was admitted this morning.'

'How is she?'

The girl looked embarrassed, and I wondered if she'd been told to keep her mouth shut. She was already half-way to the door.

'Sleeping most of the time,' she said. 'The DI will probably have an up-to-date report when he comes back.'

I had to be satisfied with that, and I didn't have long to wait.

'Are they still here?' I asked, not feeling up to another brush with two people I had so recently thought of as friends.

'No ... and I put them right on one or two points. I think they're rather ashamed of themselves at the moment.' His phone rang. 'Good,' he said. 'Yes, right away.'

What now? I wondered.

The answer came with a knock on the door, and WPC Crosby ushering in Maxwell North.

He was the last person I expected to see. I jumped up from the chair and gave him a hug.

'Emma ... what the hell have you been up to this time?'

'How did you know I was here?'

He looked past me with his right hand outstretched. 'You've got to be Ian Foster ... Maxwell's the name ... Maxwell North. Henry insisted I got over here fast ... Detective Superintendent Henry Abbot ... he said he'd have a word with you.'

'Yes, we spoke earlier.'

'You and Henry have worked together before?' Maxwell asked.

'No. We met at Bramshill last year, and we've kept in touch. From what he'd already heard from you, Henry was convinced there was good cause for Dr Warwick's anxiety about Mrs Travers. You have heard that Mrs Travers was attacked last night?'

Maxwell turned to me. 'Why didn't you let me know?'

'Dr Warwick found Mrs Travers when she called in to see her this morning,' DI Foster explained. 'She's been with us all day.'

'And Mrs Travers?'

'She's in intensive care, still very weak and confused. It was a vicious attack.'

'Why steal my car?' I said. 'All to lose. Nothing to gain.'

'They don't know that we have the complete records here. All the incriminating evidence would have to be destroyed if they are to benefit from this scam. They know you're involved. Your car has almost certainly suffered the same fate as your flat.'

'The flat?' Maxwell looked from one of us to the other.

'Torched,' the DI said. 'No one hurt, thank God.'

Maxwell's voice faltered, showing how shaken he was. 'You're coming back to Martinsfield . . . no argument.'

'But I must see Harriet first. I'm sure she'll want someone to stay in her house until she's well enough to go home.'

'Not you,' Maxwell said firmly.

DI Foster was equally firm. 'I have already told Dr Warwick that until we have some results from our investigations, no one is permitted to see Mrs Travers.' Turning to me, he added, 'I'm sure you wouldn't want to prejudice the outcome.'

'If ensuring Harriet's peace of mind would wreck your investigations, then Heaven help us all,' I said.

There was a knock on the door and the station sergeant took a step inside. 'Can you spare a minute, Guv? Something's come up.'

'Can it wait?'

The sergeant shook his head.

'I'm sorry about this,' the DI said. 'There are one or two points we haven't covered. I'll be back as soon as possible.'

Maxwell parked himself in the chair next to mine. 'When you

were telling me about Harriet yesterday, I smelt trouble, but nothing on this scale, and I'm sure neither of us expected things to
move as fast as this,' he said. 'But, God help me, I could have been
a bit more supportive.'

'All I was asking for was an unbiased opinion, even – with luck
– a perfectly simple explanation which could have been looking
me in the face from the start. Jessica had already told me I was
being pathetic, and I was ready to believe her.'

'I thought it just *might* be another antiques scam,' he said. 'But
I must admit I was surprised when Henry took it so seriously. If I'd
had any idea that things were on the boil, you'd have been back
at Martinsfield last night.'

'And Harriet would probably be dead,' I said. 'I doubt whether
Jessica or Peter would have picked up the phone today, let alone
visit her. Jessica certainly had no intention of dropping in. Thank
goodness for golf . . . and Henry.'

Maxwell gave a wry smile. 'I didn't mention Harriet by name,'
he said, 'but I introduced the subject in a general way when we
were back in the clubhouse. Henry seemed a bit pushed for time,
and we left the club directly after lunch. There, was a message
from him on the answering machine when I got back to the
house. He had spoken to Ian Foster who suggested that it would
be a good idea to persuade you to spend a couple of weeks at
Martinsfield, and advising me to drop in here first. I rang Henry,
but got no reply. I had already gathered from his tone of voice on
the tape, that it was not a suggestion to be taken lightly.'

'I can't just leave Harriet lying in a hospital bed, probably terrified out of her skin. She trusts me. If I could just reassure her that
her interests are being taken care of . . .'

'Don't you think the police are capable of doing that?'

'I'd feel easier in my mind if I could see her – if only for a few
minutes.'

'Perhaps they can't take the risk of someone else feeling they

51

too have a need, a right even, to see Harriet.'

'Well . . . Detective Inspector Foster did make that point,' I said. 'I'm sure he knows what he's doing, and I'm equally sure that there is a local connection here somewhere. But, can't you understand? I don't want Harriet to feel I'm walking out on her.'

'You saved her life, and your involvement has lost you your flat and probably a good proportion, if not all, of the contents.'

'And your car too, I'm afraid, Dr Warwick.' DI Foster came in looking both embarrassed and annoyed. 'We should have been able to avoid that.'

I was past caring about possessions, more concerned about the constable on the desk. Whatever happened, it would take him a while to live it down.

'Don't be too hard on him,' I said, and he knew who I meant.

'Damn it all,' he said. 'The mechanic could have been intending to plant a bomb in the car and walk away. He should have checked and double-checked before he parted with that key. You could have come back for your car, found the key in the ignition and . . .' He spread his hands wide and looked at me as though he might have been sorry to see me go.

'When can I check the flat?' I said. 'I need to see what has to be done. Or, is that forbidden too?'

The hint of a smile vanished as quickly as it had appeared.

'For your own safety, you must keep away from the town for the next few days.' He glanced at Maxwell. 'Will you ring me if Dr Warwick even contemplates going outside the boundaries of Martinsfield House?'

'I haven't accepted Maxwell's invitation yet,' I said. 'I have to decide what is the right thing to do.'

'I doubt we'll have much say in this matter,' Maxwell said.

'You're quite right.' DI Foster turned back to me. 'I'm sorry. I have obtained permission for you to go with Maxwell. The only alternative is a safe house in the country.'

'You're not serious?'

'I don't think you quite appreciate the scale of this operation. You were right in thinking that antiques confiscated – or stolen – just before and during the Second World War are involved. The money wrapped up in this is phenomenal, and obviously the participants in this particular scam are completely ruthless. You will be required to follow instructions to the letter. Do I make myself clear?'

'Not entirely,' I said. 'What happens if they escape the net?'

The silence was eloquent.

Chapter 6

Maxwell, keen to get me to Martinsfield without delay, was becoming increasingly impatient.

'This attack on Harriet Travers . . . exactly when did it happen?' he asked DI Foster. 'Last night? This morning?'

'She hasn't been in any state to cope with questioning, but each time she surfaced she tried to tell WPC Crosby what had happened.'

'You told me she was very confused,' I cut in.

'And I wasn't exaggerating, believe me. Susan took notes and, cutting out the gibberish, she got the picture. It seems Mrs Travers went to sleep in her chair after watching a film on the television, and when she woke up she thought she heard a door close. She went into the hall, but everything seemed normal. She had just put on the kitchen light when she was attacked.'

'Did she see his face?' I asked.

'You take it for granted it was a man?'

'And I should know better by now. Point taken.'

'Well, you're not the only one. Susan Crosby asked the same question, and – despite the fact that a Balaclava covered most of the face – Mrs Travers was quite certain that her attacker was a man. She said that his aftershave would have knocked her out without further assistance.'

I felt that remark was a positive sign of recovery.

'She can't recall the actual blow,' he went on. 'But she did remember that the man had very piercing blue eyes.'

'Not a bad description from someone who was probably left for dead seconds later,' Maxwell said, and he looked down at his watch. 'Nearly 5 p.m. now. Say . . . about eighteen hours ago. It seems a bit pointless having road-blocks at this stage. The blue-eyed boy and his partners in crime would have been up the motorway and undercover before we were in bed last night.'

'But not those responsible for breaking into Carter's place, then torching Dr Warwick's flat, and her car,' DI Foster said.

'You're right, of course.' Maxwell had a look of intense concentration on his face. 'So . . . they have transport on tap to pick up the valuables and any documentation . . . but leave the locals to carry the can if things go wrong.'

'And things had gone wrong,' DI Foster said. 'With an apparently dead woman in the kitchen, they weren't going to hang around. They'd all want to get the hell out of there – and fast.'

'It doesn't strike me as being well planned,' I said. 'More like a local crime gone wildly wrong . . . no connection with anything on a larger scale.'

'I believe that's what we were intended to think,' DI Foster said. 'When it all misfired, they had to cut their losses. They rather spoilt the effect by taking only the pick of the collection. No, Dr Warwick, I'd go with your earlier suspicions . . . unlikely though they might have seemed. And I haven't yet told you the whole story about your car. Two local lads were found in the wreckage . . . or, what was left of them. They had probably been well-paid to waste the car, and its contents. What they didn't know was that it was already primed to ignite . . . simply thought they were on to a good thing. The hardware they were wearing on their fingers told us who they were, but that will have to be confirmed, of course. Fingerprints on the piece of headed paper we have, almost certainly belong to one of them. They are both on our files. Petty crime but never anything on this scale before.'

'So, with the elusive main operation in mind, the amount of useful information you can hope for from that conflagration is . . . zilch,' Maxwell said.

'Precisely.'

'Miss Tucker is fairly bright,' I said. 'She might be able to describe the young man she let in to the apartment block.'

'Yes. We are already on to that. That young gentleman almost certainly torched your flat, and then set up your car as an inescapable death-trap for the two youngsters. I'd like to see him behind bars before he's chosen for any further pyrotechnics.' He paused. 'I don't think I need to keep you any longer. I'll give you a number to ring if you have the slightest hint of trouble, and I'll also be in touch with Henry Abbot.'

'Whatever you think necessary . . . of course,' Maxwell said, and turning to me, he added, 'I'm sorry it took this sort of mayhem to persuade you to return to Martinsfield. Madame Lambert keeps asking when you are coming back. She'll be delighted to see you.' He looked back to DI Foster to explain: 'My housekeeper.'

But the Detective Inspector had spread a large-scale map on his desk and was plotting a possible cross-country route.

'I'd avoid the motorway if I were you,' he said. 'There could be long delays. Study this route.' He indicated the winding trail he had been plotting. 'While you're settling the details, I'll have your car checked.'

'Thank you. I'd appreciate that,' Maxwell said.

'And don't be alarmed if a helicopter seems to be taking an interest in you,' the DI added. 'It may overfly the route once or twice to make sure you are not being tailed.'

If you think Emma is in real danger – enough to warrant such extreme measures – we'll go to my cottage in Brittany,' Maxwell said.

'We couldn't guarantee your safety if you left the country.'

'But you could guarantee it at Martinsfield?' Maxwell asked sceptically.

'Developments today have shown that no one connected in any way with this disgusting set-up can be regarded as being free from reprisals. Arrangements can be made for you to go to a safe house ... otherwise, you have to accept that you're taking a chance: both of you. A remote chance at this stage, I'll admit.'

'I can't see why they'd waste time on me now,' I said. 'They've eliminated the flat, and my car. They must be confident that any papers I might have had will have been burnt to ashes.'

'They took no chances with those two lads,' he said bluntly, and left us to finalize the route.

We were well clear of the town before either of us spoke a word. I think we were both in a state of shock, stunned by the horrors of the day.

I switched my thoughts to Harriet – in hospital now, and with her nearest relatives wanting to move her out of her home. Harriet was not ready for that. She still valued her independence, and she was still capable of running her life, of making her own decisions. What she needed was to be protected from the hazards which arrive unannounced ... including those which are introduced by an anonymous phone call.

'There's our chaperon,' Maxwell said.

Chaperon? My immediate thought was of Madame Lambert. I was only conscious of the helicopter's arrival when it dipped overhead. It didn't linger, but went on its way, climbing again, soon out of sight.

The winding country road had little traffic that early Sunday evening. It struck me that, in the event of trouble, we could well have been safer on the motorway.

'Maxwell,' I said, diffidently, 'you don't suppose we're being used as bait, do you?'

'I doubt it,' he said, 'but that thought had occurred to me too.'

'My briefcase contains all the original documentation of Harriet's collection, and of the valuables which had belonged to Michael and Klara,' I said, with some embarrassment. 'I should have left them with the police where they would have been safe. I haven't yet examined them all, but the police have the copies.'

'Well . . . thank God for small mercies,' he said, and put his foot down hard on the accelerator. 'If we're wiped out, at least the police will have something to remember us by.'

'I'm sorry, Maxwell. I thought they'd be safe at Martinsfield. I didn't imagine trouble on the way.'

'Neither did I,' he said. 'And I don't suppose there will be.'

Our speed dropped. We were approaching a small village, and we wound past the parked cars near the church, taking the curve of the village green slowly. Then on, past the pub and a cluster of cottages.

'We turn off at the crossroads,' Maxwell said, as the car began to climb out of the valley. 'I can't think why I agreed to use this route. We could have been home half an hour ago.'

'Home . . .' I said flatly, closing my eyes, trying to forget my apartment, and to make myself picture Martinsfield House and its gardens. But the smell of smoke was still clinging to my clothes and my hair. I visualized the scene from the door of my apartment: a desert of sodden, black ashes, and worst of all, blotting out everything else, I pictured my car and the two dead youths.

I sobbed uncontrollably.

The car slowed and stopped.

Maxwell's arms were around me, holding me close, allowing me to let go, to release the pent-up horrors which crowded my mind. He kissed my forehead, like a father comforting his child, and gradually, I surfaced.

'We must get on,' I said. 'We're behind schedule. If we don't get back on the road, the helicopter pilot will think we're in trouble.'

At the crossroads we turned left. I was looking at the map.

'Right at the next junction,' I said.

'And we'll be back at Martinsfield, ready for a stiff drink, in no time at all,' Maxwell added, squeezing my hand. 'Here . . .' He dropped his mobile phone in my lap. 'Ring Martinsfield, and tell Madame Lambert that we'll be there in fifteen minutes and we'll have dinner at eight.'

I was flattered by the housekeeper's reception of the news that I would be staying at Martinsfield for a few days. I sat back, as near to relaxed as I had been since arriving at Harriet's house that morning.

At the crossroads ahead, police were diverting the traffic down through the town of Martinsfield, to join the motorway at a different junction, leaving the bypass clear.

'May I see your driving licence please, sir?'

'What's all this about?' Maxwell said.

'Orders, sir. Only residents are being allowed through. You can go to the right, but keep your speed down. There's been a nasty accident.'

Maxwell's foot came off the accelerator when we saw an ambulance, a fire engine, two police cars, and a black saloon. A uniformed policeman directed us to pull in at the side of the road.

'There's Henry!' Maxwell said, getting out and walking across the tarmac.

I put one foot on to the grassy verge, and froze. A Jaguar, almost the twin of Maxwell's car – damaged, but not a complete wreck – had churned up the turf. The man standing beside it, dressed for Le Mans, had to be the driver, but he looked neither shaken by the crash, nor upset by the damage to his car. If someone had taken the sleek Jaguar for Maxwell's car, then this man had got off lightly. He grinned, rather pleased with himself. It was clear that he was proud of his driving skills, and that he had relished this assignment.

I looked around. 'Where's the other driver?'

'Good question.'

With, apparently, no answer.

It was then that I noticed the young woman with long brown hair swept up in a French pleat. Not quite my double, but near enough for the purpose of the operation. She was leaning against a tree, looking slightly amused. I waved, and she reciprocated.

Maxwell and the local Detective Superintendent were coming in our direction.

'Good evening, Dr Warwick.'

I remembered Henry Abbot as tall and spare, with eyes that seemed capable of looking right inside your head, watching the brain tick over, filtering the information he needed by analysing every twitch, every pause even. He could be smoothly polite: your original pussycat . . . if you like tigers. Maxwell had him sussed from the day of our first encounter, soon after my original introduction to Martinsfield. He had warned me then not to be fooled by the softly-softly approach. That seemed like another life, but it was not so very long ago. I respected Maxwell's opinion that Henry Abbot was a different man off duty, but I had yet to see him truly relaxed.

'Good evening, Mr Abbot,' I said. 'Did your helicopter get plaited, or was this intended to be a planned part of my welcome back to Martinsfield?' I could see at once that Maxwell did not appreciate my tiger baiting, and I hastened to add, 'I'm sorry. That was unforgivable, but with today's record, I'm looking for trouble at every turn . . . and from unexpected sources.'

'Hardly surprising,' Henry Abbot said, with something near a smile. 'I'll admit, we put the show on the road, partly for your benefit, and partly for our own.'

'But the stand-in took centre stage,' I said. 'Was that because we were a little later than you expected?'

'Not entirely. This was a job for a stuntman.'

'And for a woman with nerves of steel,' I said. 'Don't tell me you're recruiting from the film industry now.'

'Success depended not only on timing,' he said, 'but also on a certain dexterity in manoeuvring a vehicle in a way not encouraged on our roads. The passenger came as part of the package.'

'And the other driver?' Maxwell said.

'On his way to hospital.'

'And where is the other car?' I said. 'Can I have a look at it? I might have seen it before.'

'With the driver out of the way, no one else is going near it until bomb disposal have given the all clear,' he said. 'And now, I want you to get back into the car and finish your journey. I'll be right behind you.'

He had no sooner spoken than a small explosion, followed by a sheet of flame and writhing black smoke higher than the trees, made a living hole in the landscape.

The firemen made short work of the blaze, but no one standing near that wreck – even with experts on tap – could have survived such a swift and devastating inferno. In my mind, the word 'holocaust' surfaced, and I shuddered at the thought of the possible connection.

'We're only in the way here,' Maxwell said. 'Henry will follow us down as soon as he's sorted this lot out.'

Taking the far carriageway, he drove slowly past the fire-engine and the smoking heap of twisted metal, and then, slipping back to the left side of the road, he put his foot down.

We came off the bypass, slowing as we approached the Martinsfield estate. A uniformed constable stopped us at the gate, but stood to attention and saluted when Detective Superintendent Abbot arrived.

'You wasted no time,' Maxwell said.

'I wasn't running the show on my own,' Henry Abbot said dryly. 'It's my job now to make sure you're home safely.'

Both cars continued up the drive, arriving to a slightly puzzled and somewhat formal welcome from Madame Lambert.

Although not running the job single-handed, Henry Abbot was anxious to waste no time in getting back to the scene of the crash. He stood just inside the front door, like a racehorse waiting for the off.

'Isn't a uniformed man on the gate a bit obvious?' Maxwell said.

'Yes. I'll make sure that's dealt with at once. Until further notice, I want you both to remain inside the house. Someone may be watching your movements. I realize that it is not a comfortable situation, but if you are able to show that you are keeping to a normal routine, with luck, I think we may have seen an end to your involvement.' He turned to me. 'Ian Foster wants me to thank you for your valuable assistance, and to tell you that he'll keep you informed about the progress of Mrs Travers. That's all from Foster, but I've been asked to find out if you would agree to write a feature, based on documentation and photographs belonging to Mrs Travers . . . for publication in a national newspaper or its weekend magazine.'

'Has Mrs Travers been consulted?'

'Not yet.'

'I won't touch it without her permission.'

'But, you wouldn't be averse to taking on the work if Mrs Travers was willing for it to be published?'

'Not at all. Although writing it does not mean that it will be accepted, and I have none of the photographs here. Some are with the police . . . others with the photographer.'

'I'll deal with that,' he said. 'One of the editors was particularly interested in the idea.'

'Ignoring the photographs for the moment . . . I'm a working woman. I have another house restoration on my books. I had arranged to go down there this week. Is that vetoed too?'

He nodded.

'All the paperwork has been trashed in the fire at my apartment. That is going to entail a massive amount of extra work. You can imagine . . .'

'I can indeed.'

'They're going to think I don't want the job. Wednesday? Surely, if nothing unpleasant has happened by then . . .'

'Absolutely not. I know it must be very frustrating,' Henry said, 'but it is not *I* who set the parameters this time. I too have to obey orders.' Detective Superintendent Abbot was digging his toes in. 'Go on! Have a crack at it, Emma.'

Every trick in the book . . . and then some, I thought. Two could play at that game. I'd write the feature, but then I'd be on the war-path again.

'All right, Henry,' I said. 'I'll do my best . . . but don't expect miracles.'

Chapter 7

It was fortunate that I had been persuaded by Maxwell to leave clothes and toiletries at Martinsfield, so that I could stop over at any time. I had not expected to use them quite so soon.

Madame Lambert could not have been kinder. She knew perfectly well that there was more to my arrival than a last minute invitation. When I reached my bedroom she was already laying out my clothes for the evening, and there was a large linen bag waiting for my smoke-clogged garments. I wasn't capable of thinking clearly. I could have hugged her, but I knew Madame Lambert well enough to appreciate that she was a formal creature: efficient, loyal, and – yes – kind, in her own detached manner. But, that inbuilt reserve would always prevail.

'You make your guests feel very welcome,' I said, trying to show her how highly I rated the thoughtful preparations.

With a nod of appreciation, she left me.

I stripped to the skin, dumping everything in the bag, and unpinning my long hair so that I could wash it in the shower.

The impact of the warm water running through the lather of the shampoo, the needle-spray beating on my skin, blissful cologne soap – as fresh as a spring morning – all helped to lift my spirits.

I gave a long sigh of relief.

Stepping out of the shower, I put on my towelling robe and went into the dressing-room to dry my hair and put it up into a French pleat. I was finishing my make-up when there was a knock on the bedroom door.

'Come in,' I called, thinking it was probably Madame Lambert.

'I'm hungry . . . I don't know about you.'

It was Maxwell, now at the door of the dressing-room, and holding two glasses of what looked like chilled white wine.

'I kept it simple,' he said.

I took the glass, thankful that it wasn't one of his alcoholic stingers. 'I'll be down in ten minutes,' I said.

However, when I did get downstairs, the table was being set in a great hurry.

'Louise had arranged for us to eat on the terrace,' Maxwell said. It was the only time I had heard him use Madame Lambert's first name, and I looked at her, expecting fireworks . . . or an Arctic chill. 'I explained to her exactly what has been happening during the past twenty-four hours,' he went on. 'She and I agreed that it might not be wise for us to be so much in evidence.'

'I feel I could be the source of more trouble,' I said. 'I should not be staying here, putting you both at risk . . . and the house too.'

'Non! Non!' Madame Lambert protested, lapsing, only for a moment, into French. She was proud of her command of the English language. 'Martinsfield House owes you a great debt.'

'Well said, Louise,' Maxwell cut in.

Twice in such a brief span of time was too much for Madame Lambert. 'Monsieur, may I remind you that my name is Lambert . . . Madame Lambert. I have served your family and you for many years. Our happy relationship has been built on . . .' She hesitated for a moment, and then continued, 'on . . . mutual respect. I am not able to accept the familiarities of today . . . nor do I care to be addressed in the same way as you would address the maid.'

Maxwell looked devastated.

'Madame Lambert,' I said, 'Mr North was drawing you into the family, not intending any discourtesy . . . very much the opposite.'

'No matter,' she said. 'We understand each other. If you will please take your places at the table, the chilled soup will not remain so for much longer. It is a warm evening.'

The meal was light and delicious. For a short time it felt as though we had slipped back into normality.

'D'you mind if I ring the hospital to see how Harriet is progressing?' I said, as we walked through to the drawing-room.

'You don't need to ask. You know that.' Maxwell's tone was slightly aggrieved, not unpleasantly so, but enough to make me wonder what was wrong. I was convinced that it had nothing to do with the day's havoc.

'Maxwell . . . what is it?' I said. 'Last night, at my apartment, when you were telling me about your plans for Martinsfield . . . I felt then that you were uneasy about something.'

'My plans for Martinsfield. Yes, we need to discuss the future. But now, perhaps you'll make your phone call before the coffee goes stone cold.'

I went into the study to ring the hospital, and was put through to the ward sister who told me that Mrs Travers was comfortable, but that she would be in hospital for several days.

'How is she?' Maxwell asked when I went back into the drawing-room.

'Just the usual formula,' I said.

'As well as can be expected?'

'More or less.'

'Too early to say much more, I suppose,' he said.

The catarrhal tone of Maxwell's mobile phone rent the air.

'Blast the thing!'

I was interested to note that he had not switched it off. I thought Henry's advice, that Maxwell should keep it switched on

66

and ensure that the battery was kept fully charged, might have gone unheeded.

'Hello,' he grunted. 'Yes . . . North here. Ah . . . Henry! What can I do for you?' The puzzled look on his face gradually faded. 'Sure,' he said. 'My computer will take your disc.' There was a long gap, punctuated by a few expletives. Then, he handed the phone to me. 'Henry wants a word with you.'

'Emma, I've just heard from Ian Foster,' Henry said. 'That man Smith . . . he had a taxi to another hotel recommended by the receptionist . . . out of town, and quiet. He never got there. The taxi dropped him at the station.'

'So, the bird-watcher has flown,' I said.

'He's not the Smith whose books he claimed to have written.'

'Harriet Travers was right, then. She was convinced that he was no ornithologist.'

'And you?'

'I was trying to keep an open mind,' I said. I thought he might just be a lonely old man who needed some excuse to poddle off around the world.'

'Come . . . Emma! Indecision is not your *métier*.'

'I wanted a simple explanation. I didn't want to get involved. I'd had enough. Surely, you can understand that.'

'Yes, indeed I can,' he said with feeling. 'But it wasn't your problem. You could have walked away.'

'Not when I could see that Harriet was in such a state. And how would I feel now if I'd walked out on her? She wouldn't have been talking to a policewoman in hospital today. She would be lying in the mortuary.'

'I can't dispute that. We don't know for certain that Smith is involved in this, but the odds seem to be stacked that way. What I want from you is a picture of this man.'

'Ian Foster must have a good description. Mr Smith was interviewed this morning.'

'Only superficially. The man's story seemed genuine. It was later backed up by a phone call from his son. He said his father's memory was failing – he hinted at senility.'

'He didn't seem senile to me,' I said.

'That is *exactly* why we need your help on this, Emma. You look beneath the surface. I'm not criticizing the way this was handled. There was not a moment to waste on anything that was likely to be unproductive. It was this afternoon, when the heat was off, that Ian insisted that Smith's story should be double-checked. A few telephone calls, and it was discovered that the author of the bird books died two years ago, and that our Mr Smith was not the ornithologist he claimed to be. Using the hotel number he'd been given by Smith's son, Ian followed up the call. No record of a Smith on the list of guests. We've got to find these two. I need your help, Emma.'

'I can't think how.'

'I don't want you to come down into the town, so we can't use our usual methods, but I would like to come up to the house . . . with a disc. It gives excellent results. I've checked that it is compatible with Maxwell's computer. We can play about with the Smith image until you think it is as near as you can get. Ian is getting the receptionist at the local hotel to do the same, so that we can compare results. I'll be with you in ten minutes.'

The phone went dead, and I handed it back to Maxwell.

'So?' he said.

'He'll be here in ten minutes. He wants me to show him what Mr Smith looks like.'

'And is that likely to be so very difficult?'

'I . . . don't know,' I said. 'I have this uncomfortable feeling that Mr Smith is not as old as he would have us believe.'

'What makes you think that?'

'The picture of him in my mind *is* of an old man, and I can't remember what it was that put the doubt there.'

'Don't worry about it. Just relax. I'm convinced that it's the only way you'll get a satisfactory result.'

Detective Superintendent Henry Abbot arrived promptly, and we got down to the business of Smith's identity without delay.

'A slightly longer face,' I said, when the image came up on the screen. 'Yes. And grey hair . . . white at the temples.' I looked at it closely for a moment or two. 'The parting, I think, was the other side. That's better. The hair was wavy, in a crisp sort of way. No. Tighter than that.'

Small alterations were being made and, bit by bit, a real face began to look at me from the screen.

'What about the eyes?' Henry asked, coaxing me on.

'The space between was narrower . . . no, not as much as that. Yes . . . I think you've got it now.'

'Colour?'

'I can't remember . . . not exactly. A light greyish-blue, I think.'

The eyes looking at me had now changed.

'No. They're too light . . . too washed out.'

'Try that,' Henry said.

'Yes, that's . . . nearer,' I said, lacking complete certainty. 'But the nose is wrong.'

Henry changed the face so that it was now in profile. Following my suggestions, he juggled with the features until, quite suddenly, with the change of the eyebrows, and a slight adjustment to the chin, there was Mr Smith – profile, or full face – definitely Mr Smith.

'Well done!' Henry said, putting out a hand to pick up his car key.

'That's it!' I said, pointing to the key.

Henry and Maxwell looked at me in some surprise.

'That's . . . what?' Maxwell asked.

'The key. Your ignition key, Henry. Yesterday, when I was at the hotel, Mr Smith came down the stairs as I was on my way to the reception desk. He left his key with the receptionist. It was his hands, you see. I was anxious to see the room number on the key, otherwise it would have registered at the time that they were not the hands of an old man.'

'I'll get this down to the station. It ought to be circulated right away,' Henry said, and looking at us both apologetically, he asked, 'I'd like to come back to do one or two experiments with Smith's mug shot . . . if that's all right with you.'

He was half-way to the door, with Maxwell at his side.

'Can you tell me why you think it is necessary?' I said, flagging a bit at the thought of another session.

'This is a complex operation, and we fear you may remain on their hit list. It's for your own safety. If I can show you what this man might look like without his present disguise, or with a different one, you may be able to keep out of his way.'

'I'm sorry,' I said. 'I must have sounded very ungrateful.'

He smiled, waved a hand, and was gone.

In a little over half an hour he was back again, and the vital information had been circulated. He brought with him a copy of the original disc.

It could have been quite fun as a party game but, seeing the changes that could be carried out with relative ease, made me more than a little edgy. Dark hair, fair hair, red hair, bald, beard, moustache . . . that was only the start of it. We printed off several versions, and by the time Henry was satisfied with that day's work, we were all ready to drop.

'Can we offer you a bed for the night?' Maxwell said. 'You must be all in.'

'I appreciate the offer. Nothing I'd like more just at this moment, but my day isn't finished yet . . . still several loose ends to deal with. Good-night to you both. Make sure you lock up after me, and don't neglect any of the necessary alarm settings.

There'll be a man in plain clothes on the main gate tonight, and one on the back entrance, and I'll try to get another patrolling the grounds. If they need to contact you, it will be by phone initially. Under no circumstances unlock an outer door without prior notice. Right?'

'Agreed,' Maxwell said.

'And, if you're doubtful about the identity of any caller, say that you want to speak to me before taking any further action.'

'Belt and braces?' I said.

'Today will have taught you both that scruples just don't come into the vocabulary of the organization we are trying to crack.'

'We've got the message, Henry,' Maxwell said. He was jotting something down on a piece of writing paper. 'In case the telephone wires are cut, we both have mobile phones which we'll keep handy. Those are our numbers.'

'Thank you. Sleep well.'

Maxwell saw him out, and the sound of the bolts being pushed home reminded me of Harriet. She would understand how I was feeling. Sleep well, indeed!

'I'm spending the night in my study,' Maxwell said, on his return. 'I suggested it to Henry, and he agreed that it could be advisable tonight.'

'You look tired,' I said. 'I'll stay with you.'

'Go to bed, woman. You've had a hell of a day.'

'We can take it in turns to doze,' I said, obstinately.

He knew me well enough to recognize when there was no point in coaxing or bullying.

As usual, Madame Lambert had gone to her own quarters after the coffee had been served, and we were able to invade the kitchen where, between us, we prepared sandwiches and a flask of coffee.

'She's closed the shutters,' Maxwell said, slightly amused, and touched that she was taking no chances.

Madame Lambert knew only the bare bones of what was going on, but there were enough clues to put her on her guard.

The study shutters were also firmly closed, but, in an odd way, that made me feel like a prisoner. I said as much to Maxwell, and he pulled the cord to draw the curtains across.

It reverted at once to being a pleasant room, book-lined and with a calming atmosphere. I had never had time to study the books when they had been put back on the shelves after the renovation of the house had been completed.

'There may be something there that would be useful for your next project,' Maxwell said.

'Do I get the feeling that you could be starting to have second thoughts about the workshop project?' I said.

'Well . . . there was a message on my answering machine when I got back last night. Circumstances change.' He was trying to look unconcerned.

'It would be quite an undertaking,' I said. 'You were so enthusiastic about it last night, but if it's worrying you . . . forget it. Today has beaten us both into the ground. Perhaps you need a holiday.'

'We both came back from a holiday in Brittany a bit over a month ago. Remember?'

That was after the final touches in the resurrection of the house had been completed. Madame Lambert had gone on ahead, and we had arrived, in perfect weather, for two weeks of blissful relaxation.

'Paradise!' I said, closing my eyes, and feeling again that golden sunshine warm my skin.

'Yes. It was good, wasn't it?'

'Maxwell!' I sat on the floor at his feet. 'Please . . . don't lock me out. I know something is worrying you. You're not ill?'

'No, I'm not ill. A bit . . . uneasy, perhaps.' He cradled my face in his hands. 'You are the daughter I never had . . . and I don't want to lose you.'

'I don't understand,' I said. 'Knowing you has been one of the best things that has happened in my life.'

'But . . . how would you feel if I remarried?'

'Well! You know how to deliver a bombshell, don't you?'

There hadn't been even a hint of this at our fairly regular meetings since I'd returned to my own flat.

'You haven't answered my question.'

'Anyone I know?' I said, ignoring the prod.

'Unlikely . . . although, I have mentioned her a few times. Kate came back from India a couple of years ago, when her husband died. I knew them well, and their children, in my exploring years. There was an open invitation when I was in that part of the world. I kept the kids entertained by telling them of my adventures, and I paid for my keep by adding to the family portraits, and with other paintings.'

'You're serious about this?'

'Completely.' He produced the special licence.

'And Kate?'

'Last night's message was favourable.' He paused. 'At one time, I hoped I might persuade you to forget the age gap, but no way would I risk our incomparable relationship. We both know that will never change. There'll always be a home for you here.'

'Have you consulted Kate about that?'

'As soon as it began to look serious. I have you to consider, and she has her brood.' He paused. 'You're not mad with me?'

'Of course not. And tell Kate that, although I shall be very grateful to have a roof over my head for the next week or two, I do like my independence, and I'm not likely to become a fixture.'

'Have a sandwich,' he said nonchalantly, to show that the difficult session, which had earlier tied him in knots, had come to a satisfactory conclusion.

Chapter 8

My eyelids were drooping, and I flinched at the muted purring of the phone. In the study it was always kept at the minimum setting.

Maxwell was asleep. I glanced at my watch. 6 a.m.

'Hello.' I tried to sound bright and alert.

'Dr Warwick?'

'Who's speaking?' I asked, knowing full well who it was.

There was a slight pause, and I could hear his chuckle at the other end of the line. 'Full marks. Henry here.'

'Don't you ever go to bed?' I said.

'I had three hours. And you?'

'Don't ask.'

'Who's that?' Maxwell was surfacing.

'It's Henry.' I handed him the phone.

'Hello, Henry,' His voice was gruff. 'No sign of trouble. D'you think we're in the clear?' The reply made him surface with a jolt. 'You can't mean that we're incarcerated in this place for a *week* while you lot chase yourselves around like blue-arsed flies.'

The response was brief and, I guessed from the way Maxwell was holding the phone well away from his ear, at full volume.

'I get the message,' Maxwell said. 'You caught me at a bad moment. I suppose it will be Sunday week before we can get another round of golf?'

I was relieved at the sounds of a truce and, leaving them to it, I took myself up to my bedroom, had a shower and a change of clothes, and went down again ready to face the day.

With changes imminent, I wanted to spend as much time as possible with Maxwell, but I just couldn't begin to imagine how this could be achieved. A satisfactory article for a newspaper, or its magazine, was not the sort of thing you could throw together with the shuffling of a handful of photographs and the rehashing of old notes. Then there was all my research to repeat in time for the start of the next project. I was not forgetting Harriet . . . but I was trying very hard to forget the state of my apartment, and the fact that I no longer had a car. What had happened to my car and its two young occupants would haunt me for the rest of my life.

Maxwell came out of the morning-room. 'We're breakfasting in here,' he said. 'Would you like a full English breakfast?'

'My dear Maxwell,' I said, doing my best to suppress a shudder. 'I'll settle for freshly-squeezed orange juice, a slice of toast with butter and honey, and coffee – lashings of coffee.'

By the time we had finished, the day staff had arrived. The cook, Mrs Dunn, plump and well-scrubbed, took over the kitchen, leaving Madame Lambert free to cope with the smooth running of the house.

The two housemaids, Gail and Vicky, worked in tandem, chattering like a couple of sparrows as they dusted and polished, and ran the vacuum cleaner over the carpets. They were making a fairly good job of it all, under the eagle eye of Madame Lambert.

I wondered if they knew that the future of Martinsfield House was about to change dramatically.

Joining Maxwell in the study, I asked, 'Will you help me to sort out the material for this article I've been asked to write?'

'Of course. We could both do with something to get our teeth into. My guess is that they'll want as many illustrations of the loot as you can pack in.'

'That's my feeling too. I need those photographs. If Ian Foster can get them here today, I can check that I've chosen the most effective angle for the text.' I paused. 'I've been wondering whether it would be courting trouble to have this published under my own name.'

'Good point. I think a pseudonym would be wiser. Have a word with Foster,' Maxwell said. 'And while you're doing that, I'll look along the shelves. I know there are some good books on porcelain, and one or two on silver. I kept meaning to go through the lot . . . but, you know how it is . . . there's always something more urgent which needs attention.'

'The antiques which belonged to Harriet's brother-in-law are fully documented,' I said, 'and there's information about the furniture and other valuables which were in the house in Germany.'

'The house belonging to Michael and Klara?'

'Yes,' I said. 'And some about antiques in the shop – items which George was on the point of buying to add to his collection – but I suppose the sales fell apart when he was suddenly repatriated, only a few months before the Second World War broke out.'

'I'll clear the decks,' Maxwell said, moving a stack of his papers to a cupboard in the corner of the room. 'You ring Ian Foster. We can't budge from Martinsfield House, so he'll have to get the prints to us, and he'd better let Carter know that they may be needed for publication.'

Detective Inspector Ian Foster, after consulting Mr Carter, rang back with the promise that the photographs would be ready in the late afternoon, and that he would be bringing them himself.

I asked him to make sure that he also had Harriet's permission for the article to be written.

'Let's get Harriet's collection dealt with first,' I said. 'That should be fairly straightforward, and I know we'll be able to link those up with photographs.'

It was fascinating to identify the provenance with a known piece of furniture. The police would have no difficulty in identifying the property stolen from Harriet's house.

George's old records were quite a different matter. There was a great deal of information – some on odd scraps of paper – but we needed the photographs before we could go much further.

'There's an envelope tucked in here,' Maxwell said, putting his fingers in the flap at the back of the file. 'Looks like a letter that's never been opened.'

'What's the postmark?'

'Can't make it out. George VI stamp. Do we open it?'

'I don't think Harriet would object,' I said. 'It might be important.'

'Well, if it's a *billet-doux* from George's sweetheart, he was past caring a long time ago,' Maxwell said, and opened the faded envelope and slid out the flimsy piece of paper.

'It's from Michael. When this was written, he and Klara were in Liverpool, on their way to the USA.'

'I suppose it must have arrived after George had joined his regiment,' I said. 'He went some time before war was declared.'

'I wish I'd kept up my German.' Maxwell puzzled over the unfamiliar script. He gave a long, low whistle. 'This looks as though it could be very interesting.'

'Tell me!' I pleaded.

'Is there anything in those records about a small lacquer cabinet?'

'You mean, the only joker in the pack? The fake?' I laughed. 'Yes, all the details are here. Harriet showed it to me on Saturday. It's in one of the bedrooms, the one Harriet uses: a charming piece of furniture, even down to the forged Versailles identity mark. Harriet told me that it was sold to George as a repro, and he accepted it as such, at a price which reflected its lack of pedigree. He too must have thought it an attractive piece of furniture. Harriet has great affection for it herself.'

'And it's still there?'

'When I went over the house with the police yesterday, yes, it was in Harriet's bedroom. I'm certain about that. As far as I could see, nothing upstairs had been touched.'

'Well, unless my reading of this scrap of paper is wide of the mark, that cabinet is no fake. It was sold to George for peanuts and this letter explains why. Michael is telling George not to sell the cabinet, that it is the genuine article, and is intended as a token of their gratitude for all he had done for them.'

'Wow!' I gasped. 'We'd better take a copy of that, and give it to Ian Foster this afternoon.'

'You like him . . . don't you?' Maxwell said.

'What a question! After an acquaintance of about six hours all I can say is that I don't *dislike* the man.'

I didn't appreciate being put on the spot.

'My dearest Emma, you've been long enough on your own,' he said firmly. 'You have brought interest, and laughter and companionship, and love into my life. I want to see you happily married. I owe you so much.'

'You exaggerate!'

'Look at the estate. Look at the house. Come outside with me, and really look at it. And look at me. I've said it many times. You are the daughter I never had. You brought me back into the real world . . . made me feel that it wasn't too late to make a life. There's no way you can say that I exaggerate.'

When Maxwell got the bit between his teeth, there was no stopping him. He took me out to the terrace at the back of the house, and down the long walk.

'Now . . . turn around,' he said, holding my shoulders, standing behind me. 'But, first . . . close your eyes. Picture what it was like before you began to bring it back to life.'

A shiver went down my spine.

'Open your eyes and look at it now,' he said.

The proportions of the handsome Georgian architecture, as fresh and impressive as when the house was newly built, made an impact which the final days of the restoration had never totally achieved. The beauty of the scene from that viewpoint was breathtaking.

'So? Did I exaggerate?' Maxwell said at last.

'Not this time.' I shook my head slowly. 'But, I was only one small part of the team.'

'The brains . . . the inspiration . . . the goad, when you thought the work was not progressing fast enough. The comforter, when despite all the hard work – things went wrong. The first one to praise the expertise, the work well done, even in the smallest detail. Nothing was overlooked. After the initial hiccups, everyone on the site was absorbed in the work, and happy doing it.'

'There! You're at it again,' I protested. 'You and I, we planned things *together*.'

'You forget. I wasn't around all the time. I was tied up with the television crew, and I spent part of the time in France. And when I wasn't away, I was in the studio. My painting took up a lot of time, especially when I began experimenting with water-colours.'

I smiled. 'I never did appreciate the smell of the oils. Have you done anything new recently?'

He shook his head. 'Other things on my mind.'

He put an arm around my shoulders and we walked back to the house in silence.

We climbed the steps to the terrace and went into the house. Clipped on to my belt, my mobile phone rang as we reached the study.

'Hello,' I said.

'Emma! I've just heard you've been out in the grounds.'

No mistaking Henry's voice.

'Yes. That's right, Henry. A breath of fresh air.'

The next few words were not intended for my ears, but I got the gist of his feelings about the matter.

'Don't you realize that anyone wanting you permanently out of circulation, could have picked you off . . . like a couple of wayward doves?'

I was silent for a few moments.

'Are you there?' Henry's voice was agitated.

'Yes,' I said. 'Henry, I'm sorry. We slipped up. It won't happen again.'

He grunted.

'Anything new?' I asked.

'Nothing I can repeat, except that Mrs Travers seems to be making a good recovery.'

'If she feels like coming here for a bit of convalescence, is that all right with you?' I asked.

'Give it until at least the end of this week. I'll be in touch in the meantime . . . and, don't go strolling around the garden again. It's not good for my blood pressure. Give my best to Maxwell.'

'Thank you, Henry. Goodbye.'

'What did Henry want?' Maxwell asked.

'He sends you his best, but was angry with us for going outside . . . said we could have been picked off like a couple of wayward doves.'

'I'll give him bloody doves! I took it for granted that, during the day, the confines of Martinsfield House also included the grounds.'

'Don't be angry,' I said. 'One of the duty policemen must have let him know that we were out and about. If there is a risk, you'd expect him to react, wouldn't you?'

'Oh, Henry's all right . . . but he makes too much fuss.'

'It wouldn't do his reputation much good if we got shot,' I said. 'I'll get us some coffee.'

I didn't pick up the house phone, but went to the kitchen and found Mrs Dunn. 'Any chance of a pot of coffee?' I said.

'I saw you coming in,' she said, smiling broadly. 'It's all ready. And I was going to ask what you'd like for lunch.'

'When I was working here, it was always a glass of wine and a sandwich,' I said. 'And, perhaps, some fruit.'

'That's what I thought. I'll leave it in the dining-room for you . . . and I believe you have a visitor coming.'

'Yes, late afternoon,' I said.

'Well, I'll leave you a tray set for tea, in case you need it, and there's plenty of food if your guest stays for dinner.' She hesitated. 'There was a man on the gate this morning. Nothing wrong, is there?'

'Nothing that need worry you,' I said. 'Just let Mr North know if you should see any strangers in the grounds.'

'I suppose they've had vandals in the town again.'

'Something like that,' I said, and picking up the tray, I took it back to the study.

Maxwell was going through two large books crammed with illustrations, and he looked up as I came into the room.

'Mrs Dunn was very curious to know the reason for the man on the gate,' I said.

'And what did you tell her?'

'She suggested vandals, and I agreed.'

'If she thinks we're after vandals, I suppose she's not so far off the mark,' he said. He was looking tired.

'It might be a good idea for you to have a rest after lunch,' I said. 'I don't suppose Ian Foster will be here until four or five at the earliest.'

I was surprised that he agreed so readily.

Chapter 9

Exploring various angles for the newspaper feature had swallowed up most of the afternoon. I had worked out two possible angles to follow: one dealing only with items stolen from Harriet – not naming her, of course; the other covering a wider field, but making no reference to our local robbery – a 'where are they now' feature – hoping that it might at least put people on their guard, and, with luck, produce fresh evidence. I had received no definite guidelines from the police, but I hoped that Ian Foster was going to fill in the gaps.

Maxwell had slept for part of the afternoon, but he was downstairs when Ian arrived with the photographs.

'I'll let him in,' he said. 'You make the tea.'

True to her promise, Mrs Dunn had left the tray set for tea, with some wicked-looking little cakes, which vanished like snow in summer when the men set eyes on them.

With tea out of the way, we went into the study where Ian spread the prints across Maxwell's desk and an adjoining table.

'Carter's made a good job of these,' he said. 'And here's a note from Mrs Travers giving you permission to use the documents and prints for your newspaper article.'

'Any news of Harriet's property?' I asked, as we sifted through, and matched the individual prints with the appropriate documents.

'Not a sniff,' he said. 'It's infuriating, but not altogether surprising. Allowing for the barbaric nature of those at the top, one whisper from any underling, and he's dead. It's become clear that they don't even have to do anything wrong. If they've done their job, and they're of no further use, they're expendable.'

'Like the two young men in my car,' I said bleakly.

'Exactly. One of the reasons why we thought it advisable for you to go to a safe house. There's still time for you to change your mind.'

'I have to keep reminding people that I'm a working woman,' I said.

'Well, if you want to stay that way, keep your head down for a while.'

'Have a look at what Maxwell found at the back of one of our files,' I said, handing him the letter which had remained unopened for over sixty years.

'Well . . . I'm blessed!' He clearly had no difficulty in translation. 'That should give Harriet Travers something to smile about.'

'Will you go in to see her, and tell her about it?' I asked, showing him the appropriate photograph.

'You bet I will! It'll perk her up to have a bit of good news.'

For a while, we talked about the format of the piece I was going to write. It looked as though I was going to end up with a *mélange* of the two versions. We agreed . . . no by-line.

'You look tired, Ian,' Maxwell said.

'I didn't get to bed last night, and on Saturday night we were dealing with a crowd of drunks, and I didn't get my head down until about three a.m.' He stifled a yawn. 'I must make a move.'

'Stay the night,' Maxwell said.

'Thank you, but no. It won't take me long to drive back. And I must get in early tomorrow.'

'Yes, I understand,' Maxwell said. 'Your wife must see little enough of you as it is.'

'My wife would have agreed with you there. She left me four years ago,' Ian said, and I could have kicked Maxwell. To me, it was an obvious check on Ian's marital status. However, it was also obvious that Ian was in no fit state to drive anywhere.

'Do stay,' I said. 'You look ready to drop.'

'It's very tempting.'

'Then, that's settled,' Maxwell insisted. 'You wouldn't approve of a member of the public driving in similar circumstances.' He was already at the door, on his way to see Madame Lambert and Mrs Dunn. 'My guess is that my cook and housekeeper are two jumps ahead of us.'

'But . . . I have nothing with me . . .'

'No problem,' I said. 'Madame Lambert is prepared for any such eventuality. As I have discovered in the past, in similar circumstances, everything you need will be in your room.'

'Are you going to stay on here?' It seemed to be Ian's turn to do the probing.

'For the next couple of weeks,' I said. 'Perhaps longer. My apartment is a complete disaster area, as you well know.'

He nodded. 'They made a thorough job of it, but the fire crew did a great salvage operation. Some of the books which were under glass appear to have survived – the ones that were away from the main blast of the heat.'

'And the other rooms?'

'All turned over. Mainly smoke damage.'

'When can I see it for myself?'

'If there's no sign of further activity, probably by the end of this week. When do you expect to finish the newspaper article?'

'With Maxwell's help, I've got it all mapped out. Now that you've given me a better idea of what is required, with luck, I'll finish it tomorrow.'

'Great! Henry will pick it up. It has to be vetted by the head of this operation before it goes to the editor. In fact, it'll be in the newspaper, not in the magazine. All a question of what has already gone to press, and taking advantage of the more adaptable newspaper, where this can be slotted in at once.'

Maxwell returned with a grin on his face.

'I tell you . . . everything was already organized. We could all do with a good night's sleep. I'll take you up to your room, Ian, and I suggest we all meet down here in . . .' He checked the time. 'In half an hour. Time for a snifter before dinner.'

Maxwell was in the drawing-room when I came downstairs again.

'You seem to get on well with him,' he said, with more than a touch of approval. I knew what he was up to.

'And you think he's the answer to tidying up the loose ends. It isn't catching, you know,' I protested. 'I'm my own person. I *won't* be manipulated. Forget it, Maxwell.'

I was relieved by Ian's arrival, which cut short any further exploration of the subject.

'Madame Lambert . . . how does she do it?' he said, raising his glass. 'Here's to perfection!'

Maxwell and I raised our glasses in agreement. We were all a little more relaxed, but Ian was still very much on duty.

'Can I take it that, with the exception of this room, all the doors and windows have been secured, and that the alarm system is fully operational?' he said.

Maxwell put his glass down. 'Mrs Dunn will have gone home by now. I suppose a double-check wouldn't hurt.'

'I'll come with you,' Ian said, 'but, we'll make this room secure first.'

I watched them closing and locking the windows and the big double doors leading out on to the terrace, and I began to wish that I had gone to the offered safe house, which would have kept this lovely Georgian house, and its owner, free from further risk.

Ten minutes had passed before Maxwell and Ian returned.

They had had a word with Madame Lambert, to give her the choice of remaining, or leaving with Ian in the morning. She had insisted upon staying, but agreed that Mrs Dunn and the two maids should not be put at risk. Maxwell had suggested that she should phone Mrs Dunn and the girls first thing in the morning and tell them that we had been called away unexpectedly, and would probably not be back for at least a week. In the meantime, they could regard it as extra holiday.

Madame Lambert appeared at the door to call us to the table.

Mrs Dunn had indeed made a special effort. The chilled vichyssoise, with a herb and lemon garnish, was exactly what that warm evening called for. This, followed by roast duck with a sharp, morello-cherry sauce, tiny new potatoes and fresh garden peas, and we were beyond thinking of anything more serious than the wine, which Maxwell and Ian discussed with knowledge and enthusiasm, and I simply enjoyed.

Madame Lambert next produced the cheeseboard, followed by a simple fruit salad with cream.

'I now understand why our safe house was rejected,' Ian commented drily, sitting back in his chair.

'Before we have coffee, I'd like to ring the hospital,' I said.

'I'll do it, if you don't mind,' Ian said, and glancing at Maxwell, he added, 'All right with you?'

Maxwell nodded, without much enthusiasm. 'There's a phone in the study.'

'I'll use my mobile,' Ian said, and crossed the room, whether to avoid us getting the gist of the conversation, or out of belated courtesy, it was impossible to know.

This is the creature I'm supposed to be getting on with so splendidly, I thought. Judging from the expression on Maxwell's face, he too was having second thoughts.

'Well?' Maxwell said coolly, when Ian joined us again.

'Not such a good day, I'm afraid, but that's not unusual with concussion. They're keeping her in intensive care, and the sister suggests you ring in the morning.'

'Coffee in the drawing-room,' Maxwell said, pulling my chair back. 'And then, I think we'll all be ready to make tracks, and hope for a quiet night.'

'I must be away by six a.m. at the latest,' Ian said. 'I'm afraid that means that someone will have to reactivate the security system.'

'You'll need a good breakfast before you go,' Maxwell said. 'I'm always awake at that time.'

'All dealt with. Although I told her that I was not a breakfaster, your housekeeper insisted that I accept a tray. She brought it to my room as I was coming down to dinner. Everything I could possibly need is there. All I have to do is to pour water on to the coffee.'

'And talking of coffee,' Maxwell said, ushering us across the wide hall into the drawing-room, 'how do you like yours, Ian?'

'Black, please.'

Conversation was on the wane, and someone had to make the first move.

'Maxwell,' I said. 'Ian is nearly dead on his feet. He has to be off early tomorrow, and we must make an early start too. I'd like Henry to be able to pick up the finished article, with the illustrations, by mid-afternoon.'

'D'you really think you can finish it by then?' Ian said.

'I know now exactly what is needed. As I mentioned earlier, Maxwell and I did a lot of the groundwork this morning, and I spent the afternoon planning different approaches to the subject, two of which are now going to be combined. Yes, there's a fair chance I'll be able to cross that off the list tomorrow, and then I can concentrate on my own research. I must ring the clients, otherwise they'll think I'm losing interest in their house.'

'Another job like this?' Ian asked casually.

'Oh, no. Martinsfield is unique.'

'A magnet for trouble?'

'Not any more!' I was angry that he should link Martinsfield with the present troubles. 'If some idiot hadn't sent the decoy car up the motorway, and off at the exit that coaxed the car that was tailing it in the direction of Martinsfield, I doubt that any connection with this house would have been made. But the car crash was near enough to Martinsfield for the name to ring a few bells . . . unless . . .' A half-formed idea was nudging its way into my mind. 'Unless the driver used his mobile to warn someone to search elsewhere, to tell them that he'd been following the wrong car.'

'Of course! Setting off the incendiary device. An electronic signal. *That's* how it was done,' Ian said, sidetracking. 'Henry told me they had one hell of a job to get the guy out of the car. In the end cutting equipment had to be used. The guy was almost out of his mind with pain, but he insisted he'd been told to stay in the car until someone arrived to pick him up and take him to a private hospital. I believe there was an electronic trigger to jam the doors and set off a timer for the incendiary bomb, a simple device which was intended to wipe out both car and driver. The same with your car, of course.'

'All planned in advance,' I said. 'Report that the job has been done, or that it's gone wrong . . . and the result is the same, either way. What sort of a mind can dole out such butchery?'

'Ian,' Maxwell cut in. 'I can see now that I made a great mistake in asking Emma to come back here. There's no way the local police can make this place safe. If you took her with you in the morning, could you still find her a place in a safe house until it all blows over?'

'I'll have a word with Henry . . .' Ian began, but I cut in.

'Isn't anyone going to have a word with me. . . ?'

'Emma, I made a big mistake, and I've got to put it right,' Maxwell insisted.

'Not you, my dear.' I turned back to Ian. 'It's obvious that this is part of a larger, and carefully planned, operation. The robbery at Harriet's house was not an isolated incident. If my guess is right, the top brass must have accepted that all concerned had to be considered expendable, in one way or another . . . on both sides of the contest.'

'Aren't you forgetting that yesterday you were offered accommodation at a safe house?' Ian said.

'Discounting it, perhaps. In my job, even one week out of circulation can be a disaster, especially at the start of something new.'

'It depends where your priorities are, I suppose,' he said curtly.

'It's an unpleasant feeling that there might be someone out there, watching us.' Maxwell had gone over to one of the windows and had drawn back the curtain just enough to see down the moonlit garden. 'There's someone over there, behind that bank of shrubs,' he said. 'He's just lit a cigarette.'

'My God!' Ian crossed the room and dragged the curtain over the window. 'Are you trying to get yourself killed? Get back to the other side of the room.' He was already in contact with someone. 'Is one of them patrolling south of the house?' There was silence for a few moments. 'Right . . . check him out . . . and tell him if I see him smoking again on duty, he'll be back on the beat. I'll be here for the night.' There was another pause, longer this time, and then he added, 'I want to be informed at the first sign of anything suspicious, however trivial you think it may be. Just buzz me. If you don't speak, I'll know you're in trouble.'

'Are you poaching on Henry's patch?' Maxwell asked.

'A combined operation.'

'Then, your visit was not solely for the purpose of getting the prints delivered?'

'You could assume that,' Ian said blandly.

'And you had no intention of returning to your patch tonight or of sleeping?'

89

'There was that possibility.'

'Has Madame Lambert been told that something could happen tonight?' I said.

Ian nodded. 'When she brought my breakfast tray, I told her that she would be warned of any immediate danger.'

'We should be safe enough in the house,' Maxwell said.

'The firearms these people use could cut through the walls like a warm knife through butter. But, of course, if you want to let them do it the easy way, you pull back the curtain and stand in the frame with the light behind you.'

There was a grunt from Maxwell, and Ian continued, 'To make things more difficult for anyone planning trouble, I have agreed that assorted house lights will be switched on, and off again later, at varying times during the hours of darkness. This should make it more of a problem for anyone to calculate how many people are in the house, and exactly where they are.'

'And also keep us on our toes,' I said.

'There should be a warning signal if things look like hotting up. There's no reason why you shouldn't both go to bed . . . probably not undress . . . get into something casual and comfortable.'

'I couldn't sleep.' I said, 'but I'll go up and change into a track suit.'

'A good idea,' Maxwell said. 'You go first. I'll come and get you if the balloon goes up.'

I went up to my room, resolving never again to get involved in other people's troubles. I closed the curtains and put on the bedroom light, and the bathroom too. When I had changed and was ready to go downstairs, I switched off the bathroom light, also the centre light in the bedroom, but left the bedside lamps on.

Maxwell was the next to disappear. The afternoon nap had done him good. Watching him climbing the stairs, I couldn't help wondering how his life would change when he married Kate. I was looking forward to meeting her.

'He's a tough old bird,' Ian said.

'Don't let him hear you call him that!'

'Why? He's not sensitive about his age, is he?'

'Why should he be?' I said, and changed the subject, trying – without success – to make him open up about the large-scale operation.

He backtracked. 'You and Maxwell . . . I can't quite make you out. You're very close, aren't you?'

'He's old enough to be my father.'

'That's not what I asked.'

'But since we first met that's how it's been,' I said. 'Just father and daughter, and that's how I hope it will stay. There are changes in the wind, but you must let him tell you . . .'

He signalled to me that Maxwell was coming down the stairs.

Chapter 10

Maxwell came into the drawing-room and looked from me to Ian. There was the trace of a smile on his face, but he said nothing.

'There's no activity out there, and there probably won't be any,' Ian said. 'Why not try to get a bit of sleep, both of you?'

Earlier, at his suggestion, we had agreed that it would be best to keep the hall and staircase well lit, changing other lights in a fairly haphazard way, leaving some on for only a few minutes, with others staying on for an hour or more, to give the impression of a number of guests, some not sleeping as well as others.

'They'll think we have a pretty incontinent lot staying here,' Maxwell remarked.

The three of us were beginning to think that our precautions had been a bit of a joke, when Ian got a warning message from his sergeant outside, and our smug satisfaction evaporated.

'It could be a false alarm,' Ian said, but we'd better be ready for anything. The cellar could become a trap. The corridors on the first floor are probably as safe as anywhere else.'

'I'll get Madame Lambert,' I said, and ran up the two flights of stairs to the second floor.

Madame Lambert was awake when I tapped on her door. She was lying on top of the duvet, fully clothed, and clearly prepared for the worst. The bedside light, well away from the window, was switched on, and we decided to leave it that way.

'There's a crazy man on the loose, and he might have a gun,' I said. (The understatement of the year, if we were being targeted.) 'It's just possible that he has got into the grounds. I'm sure you understand that Mr Foster doesn't want us to take any chances.'

'*Je comprends absolument!*' she said, and her lapse into her own language made me realize that she was more shaken than she appeared to be.

'The corridor on the first floor will give us a certain amount of shelter,' I said.

The men were at the bottom of the upper flight of stairs, waiting for us with a barrage of cushions from the drawing-room. They made sure we were reasonably comfortable before going on a tour of the house.

Madame Lambert and I remained where we were, feeling a bit foolish. However, I could not help reflecting on the previous day's record. Any involvement, however insignificant, had meant that the slate must be wiped clean. Was it going to be the same with Martinsfield?

We listened.

Not a sound.

The silence seemed to hold a threat of impending trouble, rather than a touch of comfort.

After the previous day's carnage, I could understand the extreme caution but, as time passed and no violence materialized, both Madame Lambert and I gradually, very gradually, relaxed.

At last, Maxwell and Ian returned.

'My apologies,' Ian said. 'It was a false alarm.'

'Please, Monsieur, do not apologize,' Madame Lambert said, taking the offered hand and getting to her feet. 'Is there anything I can get for you, before I go back to my bed?'

We assured her that there was nothing we required, and Ian

took her to her bedroom door, rejoining Maxwell and me in the now dimly-lit drawing-room.

'Ian, d'you know what's going on out there?' Maxwell asked.

'There are men positioned in the grounds whose main aim is to ensure that you enjoy the sunrise.'

'Main aim . . . I get your drift.' Maxwell put his hands on my shoulders. 'Emma, you do manage to attract trouble!'

'Not by choice, believe you me!' I said sharply.

'You must have a fair number of men on the job?' Maxwell said, turning back to Ian. It was a question, not a comment. Getting no reply, he added, 'Not much of a result, so far. You're sure there isn't an informer in the pack?'

'I'm sorry. I can't discuss this with you,' Ian said. 'There is room in this international scam for every type of drop-out that society can throw up. We are not unaware of the hazards. All I can say is that if we don't come up with the goods, we'll get a lot of stick from the great British public . . . and, in that event, we'll deserve it.'

'This has been your life since you left full-time education, I suppose,' Maxwell said.

'No, I joined the force relatively late in my career.'

'And you're in the fast lane?'

'Not for me to say.' Ian looked at me, and grinned.

I knew he was thinking of the protective father/daughter relationship, and I was not amused.

'What did you do before you joined the force?' I asked.

Ian's mobile phone demanded attention. It was a convenient get out.

'I'll take this in the hall,' he said, closing the door behind him, and it was several minutes before he returned. 'Sorry about that. It was Henry. He's taking over, as from now. I leave you in good hands. It is possible that you may soon be in the clear.'

'Things are on the move, are they?' Maxwell said.

'Slight progress,' was all Ian would say.

'And when can I see Harriet?' I asked.

'I'll let you know.'

I could see that I'd have to be content with that reply, for the moment, but I didn't intend to allow things to stand still for long. I needed to be mobile, and I would have to get a new car.

'What *did* you do?' I said again, with more emphasis this time, curious at his apparent reluctance to answer the question.

'I'll tell you all about my misspent youth the next time we meet. Now, I'm going to have a shower, and do justice to Madame Lambert's breakfast tray, before I get back to base. And I suggest that you and Maxwell get some sleep, or you won't be fit to finish that feature. You'll have the editor breathing down your neck.'

'He, or she, hasn't been in touch yet,' I said.

'Well, he and Henry spent some time working out the details. It's a . . . delicate balance.'

'They could have included me. After all, I'll be writing it! It wouldn't have hurt to pick up a telephone.'

'Telephone calls can be traced,' Ian said. 'I'll be down again during the week.'

'While I'm here, what if friends want to drop in?'

'I wouldn't encourage it, but . . . if you can vouch for them . . . fine. Don't let them know that there's anything out of the ordinary going on. And, check with Henry first, otherwise they may not get past the gate.'

The dawn was just beginning to break when Ian left, going down the drive in his sleek blue Jaguar, slowly, without lights. It appeared that precautions were still being taken, but the pressure seemed to have eased a little.

Maxwell and I took Ian's advice and had a couple of hours' sleep, coming down to breakfast only a little later than usual.

It was a beautiful morning, and it seemed a crime to remain in the house, but we had no choice; the garden was still out of bounds, and the newspaper article had to be tackled. Maxwell arranged the documents and the matching photographs in a series of folders, leaving me to get on with the writing. The first draft was finished by mid-morning and, with one or two minor alterations and additions, I was able to print it by lunchtime.

Henry dropped in for a sandwich lunch and was having a drink with Maxwell when I handed over the finished work.

'Forgive me if I look through it straight away,' he said, sitting down and running his index finger down the pages, making brief comments as he progressed.

'Hm . . . struck the right note in the first paragraph.' A pause. 'I like that . . . yes, that'll make them think.' He continued to the final paragraph and, looking up at me, said, 'Right first time, in my opinion. Covers all the points we made. I'd say it is *exactly* what is needed . . . and it makes damned good reading too. And those illustrations . . . first class. An excellent bit of work, Emma.'

'Thank you, Henry. Now, can you do something for me?' I said, and I handed him three of the photographs taken by Harriet, or her husband, when they were in Germany in 1946. 'Could your people enlarge those, and get on disc the faces of the two men who are standing near the wreckage of the house, as you did with my efforts to identify Mr Smith?'

'What have you in mind?'

'I just wonder if one of them could be Smith as a young man.'

'Worth a try,' he said, and turned to Maxwell. 'Forgive me if I skip lunch. This looks interesting. I'll be in touch.'

He picked up my morning's work and the photographs and was away almost before we could draw breath.

After lunch, Maxwell went into the drawing-room to read the newspapers, leaving me to get on with my own work.

It was an afternoon of lengthy telephone calls, some of which produced information which I had originally supplied to the people involved. This was going to save me hours of further research.

I was feeling rather pleased with myself when Madame Lambert came into the study and told me that there were two visitors for me in the drawing-room: Jessica Hammond, and her brother Peter Jackson. Euphoria went into reverse.

'Does Mr North know they are here?' I asked her.

'Yes.' She was already retreating.

I wondered how they knew where I was, and supposed it was guesswork on Jessica's part. I was not looking forward to this unplanned get-together, and I went into the drawing-room ready for fireworks.

'Have *you* seen Harriet?' Jessica demanded icily.

'No.' I was equally cool. 'Have you?'

'Oh! *Why* did I involve you in this?' Jessica looked like an ill-tempered child, about to stamp her foot. I almost laughed, but there was really nothing even remotely amusing about her attitude.

Maxwell was standing at one of the windows. He turned back to face Jessica and, controlling his anger, said, 'So, you would have preferred Emma to ignore the plight of Mrs Travers. In that case, Mrs Hammond, your Aunt Harriet would now be dead. It would seem an odd preference for a devoted niece.'

'Er . . . so sorry to hear about your flat, Emma,' Peter cut in, trying to avoid further conflict. I felt sorry for him. He looked extremely embarrassed.

'Thank you,' I said, and asked casually, 'You're not at work today?' I was wondering what had persuaded him to bring Jessica to Martinsfield.

'It's been a tough time for Jess,' he said. 'I'm taking a few days off before Barry returns from New York. We were hoping to see Harriet this afternoon. I understand she's making reasonable progress, but they wouldn't let us in to see her today, and couldn't tell us when it might be possible.'

'Yes,' I said. 'I gathered that was the position.'

'But we are her nearest and dearest,' Jessica protested. 'You'd think we might be entitled to preferential treatment.'

Nearest and dearest? An inaccurate description, if ever there was one. I couldn't trust myself to make any reponse, but Maxwell accelerated their departure by telling them that they were very lucky to have reached us without having their car's windscreen shattered.

'There's trouble with vandals at the moment,' he explained briefly.

'I did wonder why the gate was manned,' Peter said, 'but I thought perhaps the police might be keeping a surreptitious eye on things after Sunday's havoc.'

'Why should they bother with us?' I said. 'Better things to do with their time.'

'Er . . . yes, I suppose you're right.' He frowned at his sister with some irritation, and turning back to me, said, 'It's time we were off. We shouldn't have dropped in without letting you know in advance. Just wanted to make sure you were all right.' And taking my hands in his, he added, 'Emma, I'm sorry for the disagreements we've had. If there's anything I can do to help with the flat . . .'

'Thank you, Peter, but everything is under control, and I think the time has come for me to move on.'

He glanced at Maxwell, and I knew exactly what Peter was thinking. He couldn't have been more wrong, but I wasn't going to tell him that. With Jessica within hearing distance, it would be like putting it on the Internet.

Chapter 11

'Well! What did you make of that?' Maxwell asked, as we watched Peter and Jessica disappearing around the bend in the drive.

'Jessica always likes to be the first with any news,' I said. 'I'm afraid, when she gets back home, my whereabouts will have widespread coverage.'

'A tiresome female,' Maxwell commented. 'I can't help wondering if she and her brother could be involved in this disgusting scam.'

'I'll admit they don't seem to have Harriet's welfare at the top of their list, but I find it difficult to believe that they would condone anything which might harm her . . . physically, that is.'

'But they might not be above accepting a large hand-out for useful information?' His bristling eyebrows met in a frown.

'Be logical, Maxwell!' I said. 'If Harriet's treasures have gone for good, Jessica and Peter will be the losers in the long run.'

'I take it Harriet has the contents of her house insured,' he said cynically.

'Probably, but I'd be prepared to bet that the cover is for nothing like today's values.'

He grunted. 'You'd better have a word with Ian. I'll speak to

Henry. They should know of this development. We'll take it from there.'

Maxwell went into the study, and I went up to my bedroom to ring Ian on my mobile, which I'd left beside my bed.

When I gave my name, I was put through to him at once, and told him of our late afternoon visitors.

'Damn the woman!' he said, 'And her stupid brother. He should have known better. I'm afraid this means that you'll have to stay under wraps at least until the weekend. I had hoped we might have seen the end of that by tomorrow.'

It was Saturday morning before we were free to go out. There had been no further panics, not even the odd false alarm. Maxwell was meeting Kate at Heathrow. She had been visiting one of her offspring in Rome, and Maxwell was intending to bring her back to Martinsfield for the remainder of the weekend, so that she and I could get acquainted. When he had gone, I decided to walk down into the town, mooch around the market, and arrange to hire a car for a couple of weeks. I hoped this would enable me to visit Harriet on Monday.

The day was hot and sunny, and I was in trousers, with a cotton shirt, a simple cotton-hat, and sun-glasses – a get-up almost guaranteed to ensure anonymity. My long hair would be obscured under the floppy-brimmed hat, and sun-glasses do tend to fudge the features.

The market was crowded, and my confidence was shattered by a voice at my shoulder.

'How pleasant to see you enjoying the market, Dr Warwick.' There was no mistaking that meticulous enunciation. Madame Lambert stood back, concern on her face. 'Oh! I have upset you?'

'Not at all. I just didn't think anyone would recognize me.'

'Not you . . . your clothes,' she said, almost whispering. 'Your secret is safe with me. It was your clothes I recognized.'

We both laughed. There hadn't been much to laugh about in recent days. However, an uncomfortable thought struck me.

'We haven't left the house empty, have we?'

Madame Lambert shook her head. 'No. Mrs Dunn insisted on coming in today, and old Mr Selby came up on his bicycle to look around the gardens. He brought two boys with him, to do a bit of weeding. He'd been turned away earlier in the week, and he was not at all pleased about that.'

I chuckled. 'Poor old Jim. I think the hill is getting a bit too much for him, but he won't give in. The contract workers have to watch it while he's around.'

'Will you come back at lunch time for a light snack?' Madame Lambert asked.

'Thank you, but no. I'm enjoying my freedom, and I want to hire a car, so don't be alarmed if you see a strange car coming up the drive. I'll probably take it for a little run first, just to get the feel of it. I'm not likely to be back until the middle of the afternoon.'

'If you should change your mind . . . a sandwich and a glass of wine?' As always, Madame Lambert covered every possibility.

I nodded my provisional acceptance as we parted, and I continued to stroll around the stalls with their brightly coloured awnings.

A voice, not far away, made me flinch: it was Desmond Lawrence, sleazy reporter on the local paper, with contacts on the nationals. We had clashed before. An encounter with him was definitely to be avoided. I decided to melt into the crowd and make for the garage away from the centre of the town, where there were always a few reliable cars available for hire.

I was on the forecourt looking at the line-up of vehicles when the owner came in my direction.

'Good morning, Bill,' I said, and he looked at me as though he had never seen me before in his life. That was a comfort. I took off my sun-glasses.

'Ah! Good morning, Dr Warwick. Didn't recognize you at first.'

I told him that I was very busy, and didn't particularly want to be recognized by people in the town, and he seemed to understand perfectly.

'I don't have my own car at the moment, and I'd like to hire something small and reliable for about two weeks. Have you anything that might suit me?'

'You're not thinking of buying, then?'

I'll swear I've seen that same tilt of the head and bright-eyed interest on a thrush set on making a deal with an unsuspecting snail. He was an excellent mechanic, but a born businessman too. It was a natural reaction on his part, and it didn't put me off.

'Could be.' It took an effort to suppress the threatening grin on my face, which would have spoilt his glow of satisfaction at seeing the chance of a sale.

'I've got just the job,' he said, taking me through to the back of the showroom. 'Nice little car. Plenty of leg room, and a decent-sized boot. Automatic transmission, and power steering. Good alarm system. Two years old. One careful owner – a local woman who's going out to Canada. Six thousand on the clock, and that's genuine.' He mentioned a price which seemed reasonable. 'How's that?'

The car looked in perfect condition. I opened the driver's door and sat inside, adjusting the seat.

'Good support for the back.' He wasn't missing a trick.

'Could be just what I need,' I said. 'But I must be sure before I make a decision. I'll think about it over lunch.'

'If you like, I'll rent it to you for two weeks. Then, if you decide to buy it, I'll knock off the rental charge,' Bill said. 'But why not give it a trial run now? Then, if you like it, I can do the paperwork while you have your lunch.'

Knowing that I was being manoeuvred, amused, rather than annoyed me. I wasn't going to be rushed into buying something

102

and regretting it later. However, I trusted Bill. He had looked after my last car during my previous stay at Martinsfield, and I felt sure he would have my welfare at heart . . . as well as his own. He had never let me down.

After a brief run through the controls, Bill waved me off.

I took the car to the bypass, quickly discovering that power steering means exactly that, but experiencing no difficulty in getting the knack. Then, on to the motorway, and enjoying every minute.

Circling the next roundabout I made my way back to the garage, and Bill came to meet me with a broad grin on his face.

'I'll hire it for two weeks,' I said, my enthusiasm difficult to disguise. 'I'll know by then if it's right for me.'

'I've already done the paperwork for the two weeks' hire,' he said smugly. 'She's a beaut, isn't she?'

'I'll tell you what I think about her in two weeks' time,' I said, checking and signing, and putting my copy of the agreement in my bag. 'And, Bill, please don't mention to anyone that you've seen me. I need time to work on my next job.'

'My lips are sealed,' he said. If you want a bit of peace and quiet, why not get some lunch at that new place just off London Road. Don't take the bypass, but go straight on and take the next turning on the right. Keep on going until you see the sign. The Cherry Tree, it's called. Run by two sisters. It's only been open for a few days, but I've heard it's very good.'

With the sun-roof open, I followed Bill's directions.

The Cherry Tree had a good car-park. Under a line of trees, there were several cars all parked together; one of them, a large black saloon, gave me the shivers. Quite illogically, I didn't want to join them, and parked at the opposite side of the restaurant, near the exit.

'I'm so sorry,' the woman standing near the door said. One of the sisters, I presumed. 'The restaurant has been taken over for some sort of meeting. It was rather forced on us at the last moment. I do apologize.' She was clearly nervous and anxious to please. 'We shouldn't have agreed to it, but the man at the end of the long table lent us the money to buy the place.' She smiled and shrugged her shoulders. 'There's always a snag, isn't there?'

I backed away from the door. My imagination was probably playing tricks, but that face was vaguely familiar.

'Actually, I came in to have a quick look and to find out when you are open,' I said, and she looked relieved as she reached for a card with a small map and details of opening on one side, and a specimen menu on the other.

I thanked her, but didn't linger, and was soon making for London Road with no plan in mind other than putting as much space as possible between me and the black saloon. Heading back to Martinsfield, I stopped in a lay-by, got out my mobile and dialled the number Henry had given me for emergencies. He could think me crazy if he liked, but even an outside chance of helping him to make contact with the opposition was worth a try.

'Henry!' I said, as the call was answered.

'Who is it?'

'Emma.'

'Are you all right?'

'Henry, it may be a false alarm. but I think the people you're after may be having a meeting at the Cherry Tree, a new restaurant just off London Road. Several cars, including a black saloon. I think I recognized one of the faces. Oh God! A black car has pulled up behind me. I'm in a lay-by on London Road, making for Martinsfield. I'm going to try to get away.'

The car went like a rocket and clearly took the occupants of the black saloon behind me by surprise. There was no attempt to follow, and I saw the possible reason in my rear mirror. There was a police car on my tail. I put my foot down even harder. The siren wailed and I was forced into the next lay-by.

The door opened, and the young man said, 'Out.'

I stayed where I was.

'Your name . . . and I'll have your driving licence.'

'Emma Warwick,' I said, and handed over the licence. 'Just listen to me for a minute . . .'

'No Miss. You listen to me . . .'

'Not Miss,' I said. 'Doctor.'

His attitude changed at once. 'An emergency?'

'Get in touch with Martinsfield police station and you may find out just how much of an emergency.'

Within two minutes I was on the road again, this time with a police escort. My hire car was having an eventful try out.

The police station car-park was almost empty.

Henry's welcome clearly impressed my escort, who departed with Henry's thanks and mine.

'The car that parked behind you has been checked,' Henry said. 'An innocent traveller.'

'Oh . . . I'm sorry, Henry. I feel such a fool.'

'You can't expect all of your hunches to bear fruit, but we haven't got the final report on this one yet.' He was looking out of the window which overlooked the car-parking area. 'I see you've got yourself another car.'

'On hire for two weeks, then I have the option to buy.'

'I understand from your escort that it's quite a nippy little number.'

'Well . . . I was in a hurry.'

'Don't make a habit of it. We're hot on speeding. But, getting back to basics . . . the face – was it by any chance a variation on Smith's mug shot?'

'No. And yet, it was a face that rang a bell . . . and he had provided the cash for the two sisters to buy the Cherry Tree.'

'How the hell did you discover that?'

'Embarrassment on the part of one of the sisters. Calamity . . .

their new restaurant not available to hungry customers! And just when they needed to make a good impression. She was mortified.'

'And she actually told you that this man had funded the purchase?'

'Yes. She needed to justify the fact that the restaurant was virtually closed, and make it plain that it wasn't by choice.'

'Well, it shouldn't be too difficult to uncover that man's identity.'

'The one I thought I'd recognized was probably just a local businessman I've passed in the town once or twice,' I said. 'Henry, I'm sorry to have caused all this hassle. The man's face stirred some memory, but obviously not enough for it to float to the surface.'

'It'll come to you later. When it does, let me know.'

'Probably in the middle of the night,' I said.

'Any time. It's an outside chance, but something we can't ignore. If we're not careful, we're going to lose out on this one.'

The phone rang.

I got up from my chair and walked over to look out of the window, leaving Henry to take the call, while I admired what I now considered to be 'my car'. Bill was right. It was a real beaut!

'It's perhaps fortunate that your hat and sun-glasses effected a fair disguise,' Henry said, as he replaced the receiver. 'We've had a bit of luck. A friendly farmer co-operated by blocking the road near the Cherry Tree with a supposedly broken-down tractor and trailer, so nothing could get through from the town end. Then our boys closed the approach from London Road, but only when there were enough vehicles to make things difficult. When the cars began to leave the Cherry Tree there were irate drivers on both sides of the road, and with our boys making their presence felt, there was ample opportunity for a bit of undercover photography. They've got pictures of the Cherry Tree contingent, and their vehicles.'

'I'd like some good news to take to Harriet on Monday,' I said, crossing my fingers.

He shook his head. 'Keep it to yourself, Emma. It may have no bearing on the case at all, but there's an outside chance that you've hit the jackpot. I think you've had enough excitement for one day. I'd like you to get back to Martinsfield House.'

'Now?'

'Yes.'

'But I haven't had any lunch,' I said.

'And you won't have your dinner tonight if the wrong people catch up with you.'

I opened my mouth to protest, but I recognized that firm set of the jaw and the narrowing eyes. Henry Abbot's mind was made up. I knew him well enough to accept that he was probably right.

'You will keep me in the picture?' I said.

He smiled. 'As you seem to be setting the scene at the moment, it would be churlish to do otherwise.'

'You are expert at not answering questions.'

'There are limits on what I'm permitted to disclose.'

'I know that, Henry. But I *would* like to be able to give some good news to Harriet.'

'Well, I've been invited to dine at Martinsfield House this evening. I can't promise, but I'm hoping for something positive by then.'

I didn't take my car through the town, but went to the bypass, and then off at the Martinsfield turning. Thankfully, no one seemed to be taking any interest in my roundabout journey.

Rounding the bend in the drive, I could see Maxwell's car parked by the front entrance. I drove past and, with my old car keys, triggered the gadget that opened up one of the garages, and put the new car away.

A voice behind me made me jump.

'That was a bit quick, wasn't it?' Maxwell said, eyeing my car.

'You haven't had time to look around.'

'I've hired it for two weeks, with an option to buy.'

I told him briefly what had been happening.

'So, Henry may have some news of progress when he comes this evening?'

'He's reasonably optimistic,' I said.

'Dump your things, and come and meet Kate. The agent has found a buyer for her place in London, and she'll be moving her things down here as soon as we can get it organized.'

Chapter 12

Pausing at the drawing-room door, I saw Maxwell and Kate standing on the terrace. I had formed no clear image of Kate in my mind, so I cannot imagine why it came as a surprise to see how chic she was, and how completely confident that this was where she belonged. I could see it in the way she moved, and in the gestures of her slender hands. Tall and graceful, with pale blonde hair cut by an expert, in a short, simple style, she was a beauty. No wonder Maxwell had been charmed out of his normal scepticism. His first venture into matrimony had been a disaster. His wife turned out to be an incurable drunk who spent most of her time with a selection of like-minded boyfriends, one of whom was taking her home after a night of drinking, when he took a tricky corner at speed, and killed them both. This time, I hoped that Maxwell had chosen well.

He turned his head and saw me in the doorway. 'Come on, Emma! Come and meet Kate.' But Kate was ahead of him, meeting me half-way across the room.

'Hello, Emma,' she said, putting out a hand to grasp mine, and, changing her mind, planting a kiss on my cheek. 'I've heard a lot about you – especially in the last few weeks. I feel I know you already. Oh dear! Forgive me. How trite that sounds.'

We both laughed. There was no ice to break.

'I heard of the possibility of a wedding only a week ago,' I said, 'So, I have some catching up to do.'

She smiled. 'I've known Maxwell for a great many years. We met again because I had read about the restoration of this house. It was mainly about your work, but Maxwell was mentioned, and I managed to get in touch with him. Since then, we've bumped into each other now and again in London, at picture galleries, and exhibitions. And we dined together occasionally, just as old friends. I was probably being a bit of a bore, showing him photos of the children, like any proud mother.' She gave a small gesture with her hands, as though to excuse herself. 'Well, Maxwell hadn't seen them for years, not since he had painted their portraits for the family archives. The little brutes wouldn't sit still for two minutes. How he managed to get such stunning results, I'll never know. Those portraits are amongst my most treasured possessions.'

'Have you seen any of his recent work?' I asked.

'No, that's a treat to come. I'm longing to see the exhibition in New York.'

This was news to me.

Maxwell flashed a warning glance at me. He need not have worried. I accepted that it was he who would have to tell Kate about the events of the previous weekend, and of the New York connection.

Kate seemed anxious to fill in the blanks for me. 'Maxwell told me about you, and how, despite the horrendous troubles in the area at the time, you had transformed the estate,' she said. 'I must admit I envied him this "daughter". My brood are all male.' She shook her head slowly, smiling to herself. 'Maxwell and I certainly had no thoughts of marriage then. I think the idea came as something of a shock to us both.'

'Nevertheless . . . we were married this morning,' Maxwell said complacently.

I gasped, although, when he'd shown me the licence I should have guessed that he was planning something like this.

'Maxwell!' Kate said, shaking her head and raising her eyes to the heavens. 'You have the tact of a ten-year-old!'

Maxwell appeared to have met his match.

'I'm so happy for you both,' I said, and kissed them.

With the flourish of a magician, Maxwell produced a bottle of champagne and three glasses, and I proposed the toast, wishing them health, and a long and happy life together. This was repeated when Maxwell sent for Madame Lambert and Mrs Dunn, and two more glasses. They arrived carrying trays of lunchtime sandwiches, quite unprepared for the news. Maxwell, never the soul of tact, surpassed himself this time. I thought Madame Lambert was going to pass out when she heard the news.

'Oh! La . . . la!' She walked through to the terrace and put the tray down on one of the tables.

Maxwell handed her a glass of champagne, and gave one to Mrs Dunn, and I repeated the toast, taking only a sip myself, as I was intending to drive after lunch.

Kate followed them back to the kitchen. I guessed she hoped to smooth things over.

Maxwell looked a little put out. 'I suppose I should have told them earlier,' he said.

'You're becoming an expert at dropping bombshells.' I was determined not to let him off the hook too quickly. 'I understand that Henry has been invited to dinner tonight, otherwise I would make my exit now.'

'There's no reason for you to go.'

'Get real, Maxwell!'

'We won't be here very much in the next few weeks, if that's what is worrying you. We will be going to New York where they are having an exhibition of my recent paintings.'

'I gathered it was something like that, but I thought you hadn't done much painting lately.'

'Relatively recent, then,' he said. 'And we need to sort out what is to be done with the contents of Kate's flat. The children are going to have some of the furniture. We'll need to be up there for about a week . . . perhaps longer.'

'I take it you're not forgetting the honeymoon?' I said.

'I thought we might prolong our stay in the USA, or go over to France.'

It suddenly struck me that the options were now many and varied. The workshop idea had clearly been side-tracked, at least for the time being, and so Maxwell and Kate had no ties. I wished that Maxwell had not become involved in the investigation of the antiques scam. I feared we had not seen the end of that shambles.

'You will check with Henry before you make any booking for the USA?' I said.

'Yes, I suppose it would make sense.'

'Have you told Kate about the recent trouble?'

'Er . . . not in detail.'

'Not at all, if I know you,' I said.

He looked aggrieved. 'If anything else was going to happen, we'd have known about it by now.'

I had promised Henry that I would say nothing about my lunchtime trip to the Cherry Tree restaurant. At that moment, it was not an easy promise to keep.

'I hope you're right,' I said. 'But, you'd better give Kate a mild version of what happened, before Henry turns up this evening. He's certain to have something to say on the matter.'

Maxwell nodded, and abruptly changed the subject.

'You're not angry with me for not telling you of my plans for today?'

'Not at all.' I paused, and then asked, 'Did Kate know what you had in mind when she arrived at Heathrow?'

He stroked his chin. 'I did . . . rather. . . spring it on her.'

'And she didn't object?'

'With the special licence in my hand, for a moment, I thought I'd blown it. God! My knees turned to jelly. But, when Kate started to laugh, I knew she was going to agree.'

'You're a very lucky man,' I said. 'I hope you realize it.'

'You won't desert me, Emma?'

'You have other priorities now.'

Approaching footsteps made us change the subject and discuss my new car.

'I hope you haven't eaten all the sandwiches,' Kate said, looking rather pleased with herself.

'No, we haven't,' Maxwell said. 'But, what's making you grin like a Cheshire cat?'

'All is well in the kitchen,' she said, 'and Madame Lambert and I are going to get on splendidly.'

Maxwell grunted. 'You'd better be right . . . otherwise, I'll have to send you back.'

'Oh . . . Maxwell! You really are *impossible*! Come and eat.'

We made short work of the sandwiches and, while they were having their coffee, I went upstairs to ring Ian. I wanted to make sure that I would be able to see Harriet on Monday.

'I could take you to see her this afternoon,' he said. 'Shall I pick you up? Or, will Maxwell bring you over?'

I told him that I had hired a car, and explained why Maxwell would not be with me.

'Well! The crafty old devil!'

'If I get a move on,' I said, 'I might have time to look at my apartment to see what can be salvaged. And I want to find a place to live until I decide where I'm going next.'

'You're thinking of moving away?'

'No definite plan as yet.' I glanced at my watch. 'With luck, I can be with you in about an hour if I come on the motorway, but

I'll have to be back here in time to change for dinner. Henry's coming over, otherwise I'd have decamped today. You're sure you can afford the time?'

'Yes. I'm not actually on duty today. I just came in to keep pace with developments, and to catch up with some paperwork.'

I went downstairs to tell Maxwell and Kate what I intended to do, and assured them that I'd be back in time for dinner.

'But, I thought you and Kate were going to spend the afternoon getting to know each other,' Maxwell said.

'We'll have plenty of time for that when you've been on your honeymoon and are settling down like Darby and Joan.'

'Heaven forbid!' Kate protested. 'But you'd better get moving if you're going to be back in time for dinner.'

The traffic was fairly heavy, but there were no holdups, and I arrived at the police station within the hour.

Ian came out to meet me. 'We'd better do the hospital first,' he said. 'Don't want to arrive smelling like the residue of a bonfire.'

'Can I . . . leave the car here?' I asked, hesitantly.

'Activate the alarm, and give me the key. Don't worry. You won't lose this one.' He tapped the car's roof. 'Nice little number. Looks as though it's been well kept.'

He left the key at the desk, returning with an arrangement of flowers in a simple basketware container. 'I knew you wouldn't have time to pick up anything on your way,' he said, handing me a card to write on.

'Thank you for the thought. What do I owe you?' I said, taking out my pen and wishing Harriet well.

'Nothing,' he said, and when I began to protest, he added his own name to the card. 'There! Does that satisfy you?'

We walked the short distance to the hospital, where, despite the fact that they must have seen Ian on several occasions, our identities were checked before we were allowed to approach Harriet's room.

'Oh, Emma! How lovely to see you . . . and what beautiful flowers!' Harriet picked up the card and smiled at Ian. 'Thank you both very much.' She gave a little chuckle. 'Wasn't it amazing news about the lacquer cabinet? I'm not telling anyone else. Peter and Jessica believe it to be a fake. When I die, neither would want to give it house room.' She was pale. Her head was bandaged, and her face still showed signs of the battering she had received. 'I think I'm going to be allowed to go home next week. I don't know whether I'm pleased or frightened at the prospect.' She turned her head away. 'I don't want to live in fear . . . although . . . it may be easier now that people can accept that my original fears were not the ravings of senility.'

'I never believed that,' I said.

'That was the one gleam of hope after weeks of misery, but I blame myself for involving you in all of this. I put you in danger, and I feel responsible for the fire at your flat.' She glanced at Ian. 'Yes, I've heard about that. Not from that delightful policewoman, I hasten to add. She always pleaded ignorance when I asked for information about what was going on.'

'Ian's taking me to look at my flat this afternoon,' I said. 'I'll be over here again tomorrow, and I'll probably stay at the hotel around the corner from you, until I can find another apartment. But I must go back to Martinsfield this evening.' And I explained about Maxwell's marriage.

'Oh, my dear! Are you very upset?' she asked.

'On the contrary. Kate is absolutely right for Maxwell.'

'But, I always thought that you and he . . .'

'So did a great many other people,' I said.

There was a slight pause, and then Harriet continued with some diffidence, 'Emma . . . I suppose you wouldn't consider moving in with me . . . until you find something . . .' She stopped.

'Oh . . . no! Here I go again. I should have learnt my lesson by now.'

'If you're serious about me moving in,' I said, 'it would help me enormously, but I am right at the start of this new project. I need space to spread out the plans and all the papers and books. You'd be sick of me in a week.'

'You could have the bedroom next to mine,' she said, half to herself. 'It has its own little bathroom. Then, the room next to that is rather sparsely furnished, and the dressing-table is actually an old, and rather large, desk. That would give you a study.' She looked up at me. 'The police have a key.' She turned her head to Ian. 'You'd take Emma to see if it would do?'

'Of course.'

'Harriet, you are quite sure about this?' I said.

'If it suits you, it would solve a big problem for me.'

'I'll come in to see you tomorrow. I'll have had a chance to look around, and you'll have had a chance for second thoughts.'

'And have you any thoughts on the matter?' Harriet was looking at Ian now, weighing him up.

'Could be an admirable solution for the immediate future.' He paused, adding, 'But, before you return home, I would suggest updating the security system. You need something which will give you peace of mind in the future.'

'Yes,' she said, picking up the small notebook beside her pillow. 'Actually, it is already on my list of things to be done.' She glanced from Ian to me, and back to Ian again. 'Well, I have to have something to keep my brain active.'

'There's just one slight problem,' I said. 'It's just struck me that Jessica and Peter might object if I moved in, however briefly. They're already rather angry with me. I don't want to be the cause of family friction.'

'The arrangements I make for my own domain are my business, and mine alone,' Harriet said firmly. 'If Jessica and Peter don't

116

like what I do, that's just too bad. I wouldn't dream of interfering with their domestic affairs, and I expect the same courtesy from them.'

'Have you seen them since you came into hospital?' I asked.

'Detective Inspector Foster decided it was wiser to exclude visitors. I hoped he might be persuaded to make an exception in your case, but this is the first time the drawbridge has been lowered. And now, you must get along to see your apartment. I take it you're not thinking of going back there?'

'Not a chance,' I said. 'It's time to move on.'

'Not too far,' she said, 'or I'll think I've driven you away.'

'Not too far,' I promised, and kissed her cheek. 'Until tomorrow.'

'Nothing wrong with her brain,' Ian said, as we walked along the road in the direction of the apartment block.

Approaching the entrance, I looked up and noticed for the first time the blackened area around two of the windows.

'It's not as bad as it looks,' Ian said. 'Come on. Let's get it over with.'

The debris had gone: the broken glass, the charred remains of my filing cabinet, the wreckage of my computer system. Extensive repairs were needed. A few of the books were worth salvaging. At my feet lay precious photographs, crumpled and torn, old letters ripped into shreds. I picked up a few of the tattered pieces, and I could feel the tears trickling down my cheeks.

Ian came into the room.

'Don't touch anything else,' he said, grimly. 'It wasn't like this when I came in here yesterday.' He handed me a handkerchief. 'Here. Dry your eyes.' He was already through to the police station, but he had gone out of the room again, and I couldn't hear what was being said. When he came back moments later, I could see that there was trouble ahead.

'I want you out of here now,' he said. 'But, before you go, are

117

there any cupboards which you haven't opened?'

'No. I've looked in them all,' I said.

'Nowhere where a small incendiary bomb could be hidden?'

I froze. 'Possibly . . . the meter cupboard on the landing.'

'That's it!' He pushed me towards the corridor. 'Where's the fire alarm?'

'By the staircase.'

'Activate it . . . *now*! And get out fast.'

'And you?'

'I've got to make sure everyone is out of the building.'

'You'll need help. Some of them are not very mobile.'

'All right! Ring that bloody alarm!' he shouted. 'We'll start on this floor. You take this side. I'll do the other. And make them *move*! Don't use the lift! And yell if you need help.'

I dealt with the alarm which blasted my ears as I began to hammer on the doors and get the residents out. Half of them thought it was a false alarm, or a fault in the system, and were reluctant to move away from their television sets. The sirens heralding the arrival of the police and the fire brigade made the residents buck up their ideas, and all who had been in the building were swiftly bundled outside and accounted for. Then we were all herded into the municipal park on the other side of the road.

Fifteen minutes later a helicopter flew low over the park, and three policemen were already in place, clearing the area for a landing.

Two men, laden with equipment, jumped out before the blades had stopped whirling. They hurried through the park gates and across the road into the apartment block. By this time, the press were on the scene, strictly controlled by the police, and more police were arriving to clear the area.

Despite having recently dealt with similar incendiary devices, the two bomb-disposal experts were taking no chances. It was an hour before the helicopter rose in the air and the residents, full of questions, were allowed to return to their homes.

Ian had a police car waiting.

'Get in,' he said. 'I want to keep you away from the press.'

'The flat?' I looked back over my shoulder. 'Was it an incendiary bomb?'

'Yes. You're not out of the woods yet, I'm afraid.'

He got in beside me and told the driver to take us to an address on the other side of the town.

'Where are you taking me?' I asked.

'To my place. I had your car moved over there. A WPC in plain clothes took it. I thought you'd be able to make a quick getaway without the press on your heels.'

'But, whatever I do, it looks as though I'm going to be late for dinner.'

'The least of your troubles. Henry mentioned your escapade this morning, but didn't have time to give me the details. Something to do with this operation?'

'I'm not sure,' I said, and told him of my abortive visit to the Cherry Tree Restaurant. 'It was that vaguely familiar face that worried me. I couldn't connect a name to the face, and yet I'd swear it was someone I had seen before.'

'Maxwell's right. You're not safe to be let out on your own. I must say, I think you might have told me about this earlier.'

'I wanted to tell you, but there wasn't much opportunity, and I thought you might have put me back under wraps,' I said. 'I can't bear to have this threat hanging over my head, and I feel that Harriet could still be in danger. I've got to find Mr Smith.'

'That's our job.'

He leant forward to speak to the driver. 'Drop us here, Jock, and you get back to the station.'

We walked the last hundred yards, and it seemed that no one had followed us. Ian took me up to his flat. We went inside and he picked up my car key from the mat and dropped it into my hand.

'If only I could have contacted Maxwell last Saturday and put off our evening together,' I said.

'Meaning, you could have been at the house, with Harriet?'

'Yes.'

'And, in all probability, we would have found you both stone cold dead in the kitchen . . . perhaps not the next morning, but sometime when the devoted nephew, or his sister, managed to get around there.'

'I suppose you're right,' I said. 'But, look at the time! I promised I wouldn't be late for dinner . . . not tonight.'

'I'll let them know what's happened. You should make it by eight.' He paused. 'Emma, stay at my place tomorrow night.'

For a moment I was stunned into silence.

'I've got a spare bedroom, if that's what's worrying you,' he said. 'I don't want you to sleep in Harriet's house on your own. At least, not until the new security system is operational. I want you to remain in one piece. I rather like you that way.'

The tension seemed to drop away and I laughed, but only for a moment. The kiss on my lips silenced me.

Chapter 13

I drove back to Martinsfield feeling like a teenager who had just been kissed for the first time, but with the instincts of a woman with no illusions. The need to concentrate on the road had kept the odd mixture of emotions under control.

I was putting the car away when Maxwell and Kate, already dressed for dinner, came out of the house to greet me.

Maxwell finished closing the garage, and then gave me a huge hug. 'Emma . . . thank God you're safe!'

'We got such a shock when Ian rang,' Kate said, and there were tears in her eyes. 'You might have been killed. We promised we'd make sure you rang him the moment you got here.'

'Yes, I'll ring him right away,' I said. 'Then can you give me twenty minutes to shower and lose the smell of that apartment?'

'As long as it takes,' Kate said.

'Henry's not likely to arrive for another fifteen minutes, and he, of all people, will appreciate what you've been through today,' Maxwell said. 'He's staying the night, so there's no rush.'

I went up to my bedroom and rang Ian to let him know that I had arrived safely.

'Things are moving here,' he said, and I guessed from the background noise that there were other people in the room. 'I'll ring you in the morning. I'm relieved to hear you got back safely.'

I pulled my clothes off, popping them in the bag provided by Madame Lambert, and stood under the shower until the stale bonfire smell had vanished with the shampoo and shower gel. My hair took less than ten minutes to dry, and I put it up in a simple chignon.

Going downstairs, dressed in a floaty silk concoction I'd bought in Italy and never had occasion to wear before, I was relaxed and determined to enjoy the remainder of the evening.

'What a transformation!' Kate said. 'Oh! What I've missed, having only boys!'

'Admiration all round,' Henry said, and I all but purred.

It was a delightful evening, perhaps a little odd in the circumstances, but a happy interval in the midst of mayhem. We were chatting over coffee when Henry said to me, 'I suppose your plans for the future are a little uncertain?'

I explained that Harriet was likely to come out of hospital the following week, and that she had invited me to stay with her until I had decided on my next move.

'I hope you can make Emma see sense, Henry,' Maxwell said. 'I don't like the idea of her going back to the source of the robbery and violence.'

Henry was looking at Kate, whose shocked face indicated that Maxwell had given her an excessively watered down version of the whole ghastly business. Turning to me, he said, 'I need to have a word with you before you retire for the night.'

'Is Emma still in some sort of danger?' Kate asked.

'Possibly.'

'Henry! I've just gained an honorary daughter, and I don't intend to lose her. After the dreadful experience she's had today, you can't expect me to ignore this . . . this "possible danger".'

'I think you'll find that Emma has a mind of her own,' he said, somewhat ruefully.

'A good thing too!' she said.

'Perhaps,' he admitted, 'but it has got her into some hairy situations before now.'

'So I've been told.' She switched her attention to me. 'I really don't want to interfere, but I don't like the idea of you going back to your home town to face all the problems on your own.'

'Ian has invited me to stay at his place until the new security system has been installed in Harriet's house,' I said.

This revelation was followed by a deathly hush, and then everyone began to speak at once, stopping in mid-sentence.

'Ian did happen to assure me that he has a spare bedroom,' I said casually. 'But I must make it clear that I don't need to justify to anyone how I manage my life. I do appreciate your concern for my welfare, but this mob is not going to send me running for cover. My latest clients won't appreciate long delays because I am dodging a bunch of villains. I'll stay with Ian until Harriet's new security system is installed, by which time she is likely to be ready to return home. Then, at Harriet's invitation, I'll move in with her until her confidence returns, as I'm sure it will. It is a mutually satisfactory arrangement.'

'It sounds sensible to me,' Kate said. 'But, you will take care?'

'I hope the need for that will soon have gone. Believe me, I have no ambition to join my ancestors, but I would like to see this lot out of action for a good long spell.'

'I'll drink to that,' Henry said, lifting his brandy glass.

It was not until Maxwell and Kate had left us that Henry gave me the latest news.

'The driver of the wrecked car which you saw on your way here is recovering in a private hospital, out of harm's way – we hope. Realizing that we had rescued him from a particularly unpleasant end, he was only too happy to show his appreciation, and, at the same time, make sure of getting his revenge. He's provided the information we need to smash the whole set-up.'

'Wow! Won't Harriet be pleased to hear that?'

'You are the only person not directly involved in the operation who is being kept in the picture. It is vitally important that you repeat *nothing* of this to anyone.'

'Then, you must have a good reason for telling me,' I said.

'I have. I'm sorry to tell you that you are definitely on their hit list.'

'I rather gathered that when Maxwell brought me back here last weekend. That pile-up was intended to eliminate *me*. Yes?'

He nodded. 'One of their routine methods of getting rid of anyone who gets in their way, or is no longer useful.'

'If you are all lined-up and ready to pounce, why should I worry?'

'Everything depends upon the timing of this operation. Too soon, and we'll lose the ringleader and the inner circle. The whole purpose of the exercise would be wiped out.'

'So, what d'you want me to do?'

'It's not what *I* want you to do. I have my orders.'

'And they are. . . ?'

'That you keep to your plan to go back tomorrow, and go straight to Ian's flat. Don't visit Harriet Travers. The WPC on duty at the hospital will give her a suitable explanation. We think there is someone staying in the town, or possibly a member of the local community, who has been part of the ongoing violence, and who was probably Harriet's attacker.'

'I presume that, this time, I really am the bait?'

'Not exactly. You will be well protected, but there is no compulsion about this. You can refuse, and no one would blame you.'

'Tell me more.'

'We need to have this creature identified. We can alter your appearance. You can wander around without drawing attention to yourself. It's an outside chance, but you may see someone who could fit the bill.'

'That sounds like wishful thinking to me,' I said.

'Perhaps. But if we can clear up the local connection at the same time as we smash the rest of the outfit, it will be worth the effort.'

'And how do you change my appearance?'

'You've already seen how it can be done.'

'But what d'you intend to do with me?'

'We want to make you look older. A temporary dye, and a not very elegant bun, will make your hair look entirely different. You're going to be Ian's housekeeper . . . for a couple of days only. You'll learn how to deal with the make-up, and when you go out you'll have to wear gloves. Hands are not so easy to age.'

'And what do I wear?'

'The clothes will be provided.'

'And how do I get there? I presume I don't drive,' I said.

'You'll go by train, and get a taxi from the station. And remember that you're a stranger to the area. You'll be playing a part. Have you ever done any amateur dramatics?'

'Not since I left school.'

'Well . . . just do your best. And, if you think you've been rumbled, act your head off and make your exit . . . but fast!'

'Henry, the picture you conjure up is just too ludicrous. It would never work.'

'My dear Emma, you are being asked to do something which no one else can do. We need to find the last pieces of the jigsaw puzzle. If you feel able to help us, we'll give you all the support we can. It is not without risk, but you know that.'

'They've had everything their own way so far.'

'Then . . . you'll help us?'

'I'll do what I can, Henry.'

It was just after breakfast when Henry's car arrived, with the driver in plain clothes. Henry had already told Maxwell that I wouldn't be needing my car for a few days, and that he had made other arrangements for my journey home.

'You don't mind if I drop in later in the week to pick up some of my clothes?' I asked Kate, as we were leaving.

'You'll be welcome at any time, my dear,' she said. 'Are you sure you've got enough with you now?'

I had selected the smallest of my suitcases, packing only the absolute minimum.

'If I haven't, it'll give me a good excuse to buy something new,' I said, and they both waved us out of sight down the drive.

'I want you to put this coat on before we get near the road,' Henry said, and signalled to his driver to pull up for a moment. 'Put the hat on too . . . and these glasses.'

'You didn't see me down in the town yesterday, did you, Henry?' I said casually.

He grinned, and nodded. 'I passed the garage twice before I realized it was you on the forecourt with Bill. The idea developed from there.'

'So, I have only myself to blame,' I said, pulling the hat down over my hair, and sliding the glasses on to my nose. 'How's that?'

He chuckled. 'Ian's in for a shock.'

The transformation took place in a little back-room of a Victorian terraced house not far from the police station. Nancy Graham, a retired beautician, explained each step as my face changed before my eyes. It was fascinating and horrifying at the same time. My hair, normally dark brown, dried to a sludgy grey. The make-up was subtle but devastating, and the slightly-tinted glasses provided the final touch. I had aged a good thirty years.

Henry came in and was clearly shocked.

'Are you still willing to go ahead with this?' he asked tentatively.

'Oh . . . yes,' I said, trying to make my voice match the rest of me. 'I've got to remember to move a little more slowly, and to wear gloves to cover my hands, or simply keep them out of sight.'

I touched my cheeks. 'I trust you'll be able to find me under all of this when the time comes for me to return to normal.'

'Don't worry,' Mrs Graham said, and the confidence in her voice was reassuring. 'I'll get you back to normal in a couple of hours. Your hair will need the most attention, but it will not have been harmed, I promise you, and the colour will be exactly as before. Now, if you go behind the screen, your clothes are there, ready to put on. You'll be taking the suitcase that's there . . . not your own, that would strike the wrong note altogether. It'll be quite safe here.'

'Have you done a lot of this?' I asked.

'In a slightly different way. I worked in film studios for many years, but now that I've retired I help out in the local amateur dramatic society, but only on rare occasions am I asked to do anything like this. A far more subtle approach is needed.' She paused. 'If this is going to be needed only for a short time . . . a day or two . . . I think I'd advise you not to take it off . . . simply touch it up if necessary. I know this must sound horrifying to you, but it won't harm your skin. I'll give you a full facial when it's all over, and your rose-petal complexion will come out of the sulks.'

'And if I should make a mess of it, what then?'

'If necessary, I'll come and put it right,' she said, glancing at Henry, who nodded in agreement. 'But, if you follow the tips I've been giving you, and leave things alone unless it's absolutely vital to make some sort of adjustment, and then restrict yourself to a very light touch . . . too little rather than too much . . . then you can't go wrong. Just remember to use only the items in the little container in the sponge bag you'll find in the suitcase.' She pointed to the screen in the corner of the room.

When I saw the sad little suitcase parked beside the one I had brought with me, I had to accept that my own luggage would have been a complete give away, but no way could I be without my own sandals, and my cotton hat, trousers and shirt. It might be essential for me to ditch my disguise, and I would need to get out of the dreary clothes and relax in the evenings. I slipped them under the odd assortment already in the battered suitcase.

Changing swiftly into the brown cotton-dress and the grey three-quarter-length coat, I picked up the umbrella, a large hand-bag with well-worn handles, and the suitcase which looked as though it was ready to fall apart, and walked across to the door.

'Can you tell me where the railway station is, young man?' I asked Henry.

'You'll do,' he said.

I fumbled in the bag and brought out a purse. 'I'm not carrying very much money,' I said.

'Use Mrs Robson's voice from now on,' Henry said. 'It's too easy to slip into your own way of speaking, especially if you are annoyed about something.'

Mrs Robson. So that was now my name.

'I'm not blaming you, young man,' I said, doing my best to fit into Mrs Robson's lace-up shoes . . . and very uncomfortable they were too. 'Perhaps I've left my credit card at home . . .'

'You don't have a credit card,' Henry informed me. 'Your employer will be, paying your wages, of course. He'll make sure you have enough for your needs.' He checked his watch and noticed that I still had my own watch on my wrist. 'That will have to stay here,' he said, holding out his hand as I slipped it off. 'You can hunt for a cheap replacement on your first nose around the shops.'

'I must catch the next train and then I'll have time to go down to the shops this afternoon. Not many open on a Sunday, of course.'

'Would you like a taxi?' Henry said.

'Waste my money on a taxi when the station's only round the corner,' I said. 'I've plenty of time to get my ticket and catch the train. Good day to you both.'

My confidence was growing, but outside, in the street, it was a different matter. I suddenly felt very vulnerable. I wanted to run and hide. I stopped to take the cotton gloves out of the handbag. They were too big and the fingers were too short, but they covered my hands. I began to understand how essential it was to check every detail.

It was a slow journey with one change. Both trains stopped at every station, but I used the time to ease myself into my role, and was feeling less and less like myself with every mile.

When I got out of the train, I knew I would have to be on my guard. There was a taxi waiting.

'Can you take me to . . .' I fumbled in my bag and fished out a crumpled piece of paper with the address on it. 'It's a block of flats I think.'

'That's right, love. I'll have you there in a jiffy.'

I kept my eyes on the passers-by every inch of the way, but there was no one who caused a second glance.

'That'll be two-fifty,' the driver said, drawing up outside the flats.

'That's a lot of money for a short run like that,' I mumbled, counting the money into my gloved hand.

Ian had obviously been waiting for me to turn up. He took the suitcase out of the car and helped me to get out.

'Is that your umbrella?' he said, pointing to the back seat.

'Oh, I nearly forgot that, didn't I?'

He paid the taxi driver, and I dropped the money back in my purse.

It wasn't until we were in the flat with the door shut that he spoke again.

'I can't believe it! It *is* you, Emma?'

'I'm afraid it has to be Mrs Robson until this little episode is over.'

'But you can wash that off while you're in here, surely?'

'Not a hope. I've been told to touch it up, if necessary. It's only for a couple of days.'

'I was hoping to take you out to dinner tonight.'

'Forget it,' I said.

'I didn't realize it was going to be so . . . convincing.'

'Not much point any other way,' I said. 'I'm sorry Ian. It's no good expecting me to be Emma Warwick until I can look in the mirror and see her.' I started to laugh. 'It's ludicrous, isn't it? And I can't sit here for long. I must get out and look around the town. The few shops that open on a Sunday will give me an excuse for mooching around, watching the passers-by.'

'I've got some sandwiches. I thought you might not have had any lunch.'

We sat in the kitchen eating chicken sandwiches and drinking a dry white wine, and I could feel Ian trying not to look at me.

'Even your voice is different,' he said.

'Mr Foster, you've got to remember that I have been landed with this role right out of the blue,' I said, in Mrs Robson's voice. 'I am no actress, and so I need to work very hard to remain in character, and you must help me.'

'I'm sorry, Emma. I can't bear to see you like this. I never knew I could be so unprofessional. Is it only a week since you walked into my life?'

'You've got to help me!' I said. 'I've got a job to do. I'm going out now. Wish me luck.'

Chapter 14

There was a fair amount of activity in the covered arcade. Most of its shops were open. A likely place to pick up a cheap watch.

The bookshop to my left had several customers, but there was no one to twitch my antennae. I skipped the fancy china shop, pausing at the next in line, where rows of bright costume jewellery vied with cheap clocks and trays of watches.

'Wanting something special?' The tall, lanky youth came towards me like a stoat after a rabbit.

'Just looking, thank you,' I said primly, but he still hovered near my elbow, no doubt suspicious of my gloved hands and large bag. 'I've lost m' watch,' I added, by way of explanation. 'I can't afford anything pricey.' I turned up one of the labels. 'Well, I never! My old one cost me five bob.'

'And when was that?'

'Before this decimal rubbish came in.'

'Times have changed a bit since then,' he said. 'What about something like this . . . a tenner to you . . . battery included.'

I shook my head. 'Batteries cost money, and you never know when they're going to give out. No, I'm sorry. I don't think you've got what I want.'

I looked in the florist's shop, and then in the newsagent's, where I bought a copy of the local paper, and was beginning to come down the other side of the arcade when I heard a familiar voice.

'It's a fool's errand, Peter. You're not going to find any of the furniture here.'

'An outside chance, maybe,' he said.

'Not even that.' She lowered her voice. 'Just look at the clientele, for heaven's sake!'

I was picking over the small items spread on a baize-covered table by the door, watched by the eagle-eyed proprietress. Scowling, I turned my head to show my resentment at the remark, but also perhaps foolishly – to use this opportunity to check my disguise.

'Our apologies,' Peter said, with much embarrassment. 'My sister doesn't always think before she speaks.'

There was no sign of recognition from either of them, for which I was profoundly relieved. I turned back to the table.

'Looking for something in particular?' the woman asked.

'I want a cheap wind-up watch. I don't want to have to keep putting in new batteries.'

She picked up a watch from the display on the wall, wound it up and adjusted the hands. 'A good clear face, and a second hand.'

'That's more like it!' I picked up the label. No price. It simply had a group of letters on it. I fished in my capacious bag for the purse, intending to put it back again if I was asked to overstep the limits of Mrs Robson's budget.

There was a touch on my shoulder. 'I was extremely rude,' Jessica said. '*Please*, let me pay for that watch to show how sorry I am.'

'Oh, I couldn't do that,' I said.

'Please . . .' She seemed genuinely upset.

There was a small amount of non-verbal negotiation going on

over my head, but I pretended not to notice.

'Go on! Make her happy,' Peter said. 'Take it.'

'Well . . . I'm not one to bear a grudge.'

The watch was fastened around my wrist without any need for me to remove my cotton gloves, and I went out of the shop leaving the trio in a state of acute benevolence.

I had wasted enough time on the arcade – perhaps not entirely wasted, I had at least proved that the disguise worked – but where to go next was something of a problem. This was solved at the sight of the pavement café. I could surely get some local gossip here . . . something which might give me a shove in the right direction.

'D'you mind if I sit at your table?' I asked the elderly woman who seemed the most likely to want to chat.

'Not at all,' she said. 'Lovely day, isn't it?'

I nodded, as though a little shy. 'Only arrived here today. I'm just getting the feel of the place.'

'I see you've got a copy of the local paper,' she said. 'You mustn't think it's always like that here. Those two young lads!' She shook her head. 'I know their mothers. Always been a handful those two, but they didn't deserve to go like that. Got in with the wrong crowd. Well, you know how it is, they wouldn't be told.'

The waitress arrived with a pot of tea and two cream-cakes.

The woman looked slightly guilty. 'I always treat myself on a Sunday afternoon.'

'And why not, indeed!' I looked up at the waitress. 'I'll have a pot of tea, and one of those lovely cream-cakes.'

'Just the one?'

I nodded, turning back to my companion in gluttony. 'You were telling me about those two lads. I haven't had time to read the paper yet.'

'They'd been in and out of jobs since they left school. Mostly out. And then this newcomer down at the yard took them both

133

on. They worked long hours. But, give 'im his due, he paid them well.'

My tea arrived. I was glad to see the small pastry-fork on my plate. Eating a cream-cake with gloves on is not one of my skills.

Well . . .' she went on, dabbing at her lips, 'for a few weeks there was good money coming in, but no one seemed to know what these two were supposed to be doing exactly.' She leant towards me. 'They'd been told to keep their mouths shut.'

'Working in the office, I suppose?' I said. 'The boss wouldn't have wanted a lot of chat about his bank balance.'

'Oh, no.' She shook her head slowly. 'They'd have been no good at that. A couple of skivers.'

'On maintenance work, perhaps?'

'I wouldn't have trusted those two to pump up a bicycle tyre.'

'What sort of business is it?' I said.

'A hire firm, I think. You know . . . lorries and trucks, and small vans . . . and there are a lot of cars there too, or there were the last time I passed the place. It's down one of the roads beyond the station. The second, I think. My guess is that those two boys had to collect some of the trucks and such, and clean them up ready for the next customer. I know for a fact that they drove some of the vans . . . and that car, of course. Burnt out . . . and them with it.' She shook her head. 'Oh dear . . . it doesn't bear thinking about, does it?'

'Such a waste,' I said. 'Given too much responsibility before they were ready for it.'

'Fooling around, more likely,' she said. 'It's their mothers I feel sorry for, and the man who's trying to start up a business here.'

'Sounds quite a big business for a small town like this,' I said. 'D'you think it's likely to last?'

She sucked in some air between her teeth. I don't know. There's nobody in the yard now. Mind you, I did see the boss in the town this morning. Not in the shopping centre . . . further out.'

It was all I could do to avoid leaping in with a string of questions. I had to dampen down my reaction to this bit of news.

'I didn't recognize him at first,' she said. 'He was wearing sunglasses, and he was talking to the Detective Inspector. I wouldn't have noticed him at all if I hadn't gone out of my way to have a look at the house where that poor woman was attacked. Mr Foster's car was parked in the drive. I recognized it at once. Real class.'

Ian talking to a man who could be up to his ears in this seam. What did that signify? 'You know the Inspector, do you?' I said, casually.

'He came to give a talk at a meeting I go to each month. Very interesting it was. Answered all our questions. I asked a couple myself. He always nods to me when he sees me in the town.'

I pulled my sleeve back and looked at my watch.

'My word! How time flies. I've enjoyed our little chat, but I've still got some shopping to do.'

'I'm always here on a Sunday,' she said. 'I'll look out for you.'

Only an hour ago I would have put my life in Ian's hands. Now, it did seem possible that he had fooled us all, especially me. How was I going to face him?

Forewarned, I continued my search, keeping to the original remit. But the feeling of being part of a team had gone.

When I got back to Ian's flat there was no reply to my pressure on the door bell. I fished in my handbag for the key I had been given, and opened the door.

The smell of aftershave was overwhelming. Not Ian's style, I decided, but the air was so permeated with the cloying pong that I went around opening the windows. Ian came back in the middle of all this.

'What the hell's going on here?' he said.

'Can't you smell it? Your visitor must have put on his aftershave with a lawn sprinkler.'

He laughed. 'You don't know how disconcerting it is to hear the voice of Emma Warwick, but to see Mrs Robson looking at you.'

'Damn!' Despite my determination to maintain the image of an elderly woman, I had slipped back into my own voice. 'I must be more careful in future, mustn't I?' And I wasn't joking.

'Forget Mrs Robson for the moment,' he said. 'Anything to report?'

'Nothing spectacular. But, yes. . . there is something. It was rather odd really.'

Completely relaxed, he waited for me to continue.

'There were some shops open in the arcade. Not having any definite plan in mind, I decided to look around. I needed to buy a cheap watch, and it seemed a good place to start.' I told him then about the episode with Peter and Jessica. 'It was quite a boost for my confidence when they didn't recognize me.'

'It could have been disastrous if they had.'

'For my snooping? Yes . . . I suppose so.'

'For *you*, maybe.'

I didn't know quite how to take that remark, so I simply went on with my story, telling him about the chatty woman at the café.

'Did you get anything useful from her?' he said.

'She didn't have much sympathy for the young men who were killed in the car. She thought the flare-up was probably caused by them fooling about. It was just idle chat from a lonely old woman.'

I wanted to tell him what she had seen outside Harriet's house, but I'd been thrown by this information and needed time to do a bit more probing – to discover what it meant, if anything.

'Well, we've probably got two more days at the most,' he said. 'Can you go out again this evening?'

'I suppose so, but if I were involved in anything like this, I wouldn't be hanging around risking recognition and arrest, would you?'

'If no one was expecting you to be around, it could be the safest place,' Ian said.

'Or, of course, if you were already part of the scenery, and there was no one likely to give you away, you'd be laughing,' I said watching every muscle of his face and neck for a sign of tension, a hint of guilt.

'Have you got someone in mind?' he said.

'I'm working in the dark, and you know it.'

'Take care, Mrs Robson. God! I'll be glad when this bloody charade is over.'

'Who was your visitor?' I said.

'Visitor?'

'The aftershave freak.'

'Oh, that was the plumber. Yes, he was a bit whiffy. There was a leak from the dishwasher connection. I thought that my new housekeeper would probably object.' He paused. 'Oh God! You were thinking of Harriet's attacker?'

'It's getting to be a habit,' I said. 'I'll go out again before dinner. Shall I bring back a take-away?'

'No. I'll deal with the food,' he said. 'What time? About eight?'

'Make it a bit later. I've got to cover as much ground as I can. And now, I'd better go and patch up my war-paint,' I said, escaping to my room.

When I returned to the living-room, the little touches of my disguise restored, and my brown cotton-dress exchanged for a similar one in grey, Ian was looking out of the window, and I could see that his fists were clenched. There was no doubt that he was uptight about something.

I couldn't ignore what the woman at the café had told me that afternoon. Having to face the remote possibility that Ian was not to be trusted, left me without back-up, defenceless.

'I wish you hadn't agreed to do this,' he said.

'Why?'

'You've never come up against an organization like this before.'

'I've seen what they've done to Harriet Travers, and I've already experienced quite enough to know how inhuman they are. If I can do anything . . . *anything* . . . to help to stop them in their tracks, I'll do it.' I was shocked by the fierceness in my voice.

'Cool it!' he said. 'If you're intent on going out again, you've got to keep remembering that you're Mrs Robson, not Emma Warwick. Are you taking your mobile?'

'What would Mrs Robson do with a mobile phone?'

Chapter 15

The road outside was deserted, and the church bells had stopped ringing. I thought I'd try the park opposite my derelict apartment. It was a relatively short walk, but my feet were killing me by the time I reached the park gates. The heavy, ill-fitting, lace-up shoes were giving a most authentic touch to my portrayal of an elderly woman, but at some cost to my poor feet. I sank onto the first available seat.

A breathing space. The municipal park was well used by residents taking a short cut and avoiding the increasing traffic. The wide path branched at intervals to give equal access to all sectors of the town.

My view was blocked by people going by, or stopping to talk. So, with some reluctance, I got to my feet and walked, slowly and painfully, towards the opposite side of the park, taking care to look at every face on the way. Most of them were strangers to me, but there were also people I had known for years. I had to keep reminding myself not to show any recognition of those who knew Emma Warwick, but who would never before have seen Mrs Robson.

On impulse, I branched off towards the station and took the second turning leading to what, in earlier years, had been the old coal-yard. It had to be where the two youths had been employed.

If I was caught snooping, I would probably be classed as yet another nosy old bag, and sent on my way.

The metal gate was closed but not locked. I pushed it open, closing it behind me, and crossed the yard towards the shabby wooden building, which I took to be the office. There were two trucks parked in a bay at the far side of the yard and, behind the office, a corrugated iron structure which could be concealing several vehicles. The big double doors were securely locked and bolted, but a small door at the side of the building was open. I went inside.

There were two more trucks, parked side by side against the back wall. There was no way I could open the rear doors to look inside. But the driver's doors were not locked. I climbed into the nearest one and looked through to the back of the truck.

At first, I could see nothing. There was very little light filtering through from the narrow door at the side of the ramshackle building. I moved my head to one side of the small square opening. There was a little more light now, and I could see that the truck was loaded with furniture . . . antique furniture, by the look of it.

'And what are you doing here?'

I froze. I knew that supercilious voice.

'I'm looking for somewhere to sleep,' I said, being doubly careful to use Mrs Robson's voice as I turned to face him.

It was positively the voice of Barry Hammond: Jessica's husband, who was supposed to be in the USA. I'd swear to that, but I would never have known this man if I'd met him on the street. What I would have recognized was the face I had seen at the Cherry Tree restaurant. It was looking at me now. The photographs taken by the police as the cars had been filtered back on to the motorway had not caught that arrogance which was so much the mark of Barry Hammond. He looked younger than when I had seen him last, and I guessed he'd had some sort of face-lift. The fair hair was the most startling change, and the tinted glasses completed the transformation. With the voice as reinforcement, I could still see a vague hint of Barry Hammond. No wonder the earlier impression had been that I had seen the face in the restaurant before.

'Are you the boss here?' I said.

'Never mind who I am. I want your name and address.'

'Why?' I said indignantly.

'Because, if you give me any more trouble, I'll be going straight to the police.'

'Oh . . . don't do that!' I said. 'I haven't done any harm.'

'Your name,' he insisted.

'I'm Mrs Robson, and I haven't got an address right now,' I said, as though making a great effort to keep my dignity. 'If I had, I wouldn't be looking in your yard for somewhere to sleep.'

'Well, Mrs Robson,' he said, taking a twenty pound note out of his wallet. 'I don't like to think of anyone being without a bed for the night. Take this, and get yourself a good night's sleep. But if I see you snooping around here again, I'll take you straight to the police station. Understood?'

'It's very kind of you, I'm sure,' I said stiffly. 'But . . . I can't take your money. Just let me snuggle down in the driver's seat for tonight. I won't come back again, I promise.' If I could get rid of him I could find out exactly what was in the trucks.

'You are a very stubborn woman,' he said. 'I've got no alternative but to hand you over to the police.'

'Go on, then,' I said with a sigh, feeling that the police were the last people he would want on the scene. 'Call the police. I can doss down there as well as anywhere else, I suppose.'

'I don't want to see you in trouble,' he said. 'I'll give you another ten . . . thirty quid in all.'

I couldn't stall forever.

'Well . . . that's what I call generous,' I said, taking the money and turning to go.

'And, don't forget, you keep off my premises in future.'

I hobbled off, looking back as I closed the gate behind me.

He was still watching.

I wondered if Jessica knew that her husband was probably involved in the robbery. And where did he stand with regard to the attack on Harriet? I wondered.

My task appeared to be over. Mrs Robson was about to retire, for which I was truly thankful. But that didn't mean that Emma Warwick was quitting. There was no way I could leave Harriet with only Ian to visit her, although, whatever his role, I couldn't believe he would harm her. I tried to think of a logical reason why he should have been talking to Barry Hammond outside Harriet's house, and why he hadn't mentioned this to me.

I got back to the flat feeling absolutely exhausted. To my relief there was no sign of Ian. I grabbed my mobile phone and tapped in Henry's number.

'Hello!' He sounded as though it had not been a good day.

'Henry . . .'

'Well, hello, Mrs Robson.'

'Don't ever call me by that name again.'

'You sound . . . upset.'

'Henry, I've found the face I was looking for.'

'Well done! You should be very pleased with yourself. To be honest, I thought it would be as likely as finding snow on Mars.'

'He's Barry Hammond, Jessica Hammond's husband.'

I expected some reaction, but there was silence at the other end of the line.

'There's a lot to tell you,' I went on quickly, 'and if Ian comes in I may have to ring off.'

I told him about my meeting with the woman at the café, who had been eager to talk about the two lads and their jobs with the hire firm at the old coal-yard. 'The odd thing is, she'd seen the owner of this new business talking to Ian in the driveway at the front of Harriet's house.'

'She knew them both?' Henry cut in.

'Ian had spoken at some meeting she attended.'

'And Barry Hammond?'

'She only knew that this man was the boss of the new car and commercial vehicle hire firm near the railway station. I went to have a nose around this evening, and Barry found me in a truck parked in a shed in the yard. There wasn't much light there, but the truck was packed with antique furniture.'

'I thought you said you'd found the face from the Cherry Tree restaurant.'

'So I had. When I heard the voice behind me, that was the real giveaway. His appearance was quite a different matter. If he hadn't spoken I would simply have seen the face from the Cherry Tree. I would never have connected it with Barry Hammond. His hair was dyed and I'd be prepared to swear he's had a face-job.'

'How come he let you go?'

'I kept to the Robson image, told him I needed somewhere to sleep, and I think I got away with it. He offered me twenty pounds to get a bed for the night, and when I said I couldn't possibly accept it, he upped it to thirty. Well . . . Mrs Robson could hardly refuse that, could she?'

'I think you've got your wires crossed somewhere along the line,' Henry said. 'The yard would have been checked immediately after the robbery.'

'Nobody knew about the robbery until I arrived at Harriet's house in the middle of last Sunday morning. They had all night to get the stuff away, and it could have been brought back again a couple of days later, with anything else they'd picked up. Who would be waiting for the spoils to come back into the town, for heaven's sake? Two supposedly empty trucks, cleaned down and put under cover ready for the next customers. Harriet's antiques are probably there now . . . waiting for the dust to settle. What I want to know is, do I tell Ian about this encounter? And can I now quit the Mrs Robson role?'

'Yes, to both, I suppose.'

'You don't sound particularly confident,' I said.

'I need to do a bit of checking, and you need to keep a low profile until we can get you back to Martinsfield.'

'I've got trousers and a shirt, and some comfortable sandals, and a cotton hat. I can be Emma Warwick again after a shower . . .'I groaned. 'Oh hell! My hair! I can't do a thing about that. I don't suppose ordinary shampoo will take out the dye. Well, don't worry, I'll push it well out of sight under my cotton hat. I must drop in on Jessica, to find out if she's all right.'

'If her husband is a part of this scam, you could be running into trouble,' Henry said. 'Remember you're on Ian's patch. Wait until you can discuss it with him. And, for the umpteenth time, I must emphasize that we don't want you to run unnecessary risks.'

'You need confirmation now,' I said. 'Can you think of any other way of getting it, without sending out a warning signal and risking everything? Must rush. I'll drop in on Jessica, and I'll report back.'

The shower was welcome. My normally dark hair, tucked into a shower cap, had all the texture of an old donkey's tail, and my shoe-pinched feet had been bleeding and were gently tinting the water as it gushed down the plughole. Not exactly encouraging, but the warm water was soothing, and I emerged feeling almost human.

With my own clothes and sandals, fresh make-up – my own this time, and the cotton hat pulled down to cover my hair, I was ready to drop in on Jessica – something I would not normally have done, but she and Peter had already set the precedent by arriving at Martinsfield House on a similar fact-finding mission.

It was not yet eight o'clock, and Ian would not be expecting me to return until eight-thirty. With luck, I could find out all I needed to know and be back at his flat by then.

Approaching the Hammonds' house, I slowed down, wondering how I was going to get the information from Jessica without making the reason for my visit too obvious. A fit of indecision all but turned me away at the last moment. Without a doubt, if I hadn't been so anxious to see the whole nasty set-up crumble, I would have needed no encouragement to turn around and go back to the flat.

Oh! What the hell! I thought, quickening my pace and striding up the drive.

Jessica opened the door, her jaw falling open.

'Emma! What are *you* doing here?'

'Just passing,' I said. 'Can't stop. I had hoped to see Harriet today, but I got delayed . . .'

'They wouldn't have let you in,' she said irritably, opening the door wider and ushering me into the hall. 'I've never before known such preposterous restrictions.'

'Be reasonable, Jessica. Harriet was brutally attacked. It must take a while to get over something like that. There are times when visitors can be a bit of a pain.'

'Peter's on holiday. He went the morning after we dropped in on you at Maxwell's place, so *he's* not in the queue to see her.'

Having seen them together in the shopping arcade, I had to bite my tongue to prevent myself making some sort of comment.

'I rang the hospital yesterday to say that we would like to see Aunt Harriet,' Jessica went on, 'but was told to ring again on Monday.'

'You said "we". I didn't realize the children were home,' I said, all naïve. 'I imagine they thought it might be too much for her.'

'Not the children. They're still away at school.'

'Oh . . . is Barry back from New York?' I asked casually.

'Well . . . actually, yes.' She looked acutely embarrassed. 'He didn't want it to get around . . .'

I shrugged. 'Forgotten already,' I said. 'And I must be off. So much to do with this new project. Never enough time.'

I turned to go just as the key turned in the lock.

Barry Hammond, looking just as I had seen him about an hour earlier, was staring me in the face.

I turned my head. 'Oh, I'm sorry, Jessica. You should have told me you were expecting visitors. I'll be in touch, but probably not for a week or two. I really am up to my eyes in work.' I turned to the blond-haired man at the door – a complete stranger to me, of course. 'My apologies,' I said. 'I always seem to drop in on my friends at the wrong moment.'

With a quick flick of his wrist, he took the hat from my head, revealing my ghastly hair. Jessica gave a little squeal of horror, and Barry pushed me back into the hall and shut the door behind him.

'I thought so,' he said. 'Mrs Robson, I presume.'

'What's going on?' Jessica demanded. 'Your hair, Emma! What *have* you done to it?'

I kept my mouth firmly closed.

'I'm afraid it's going to be necessary to keep you here until I have finished what I set out to do,' Barry said. 'You might attract some attention if I put you in the cellar – too near the road. We'll try the attic. ' He poked me in the back. 'Up the stairs, and don't try any fancy tricks. Believe me, I know them all.'

'What are you doing?' Jessica asked feebly.

'Shut up, woman!' Barry was a bundle of charm, as always.

I had to keep my bearings. As I went up the first few stairs, the front of the house was to my left; turning right, it was behind me, and at the top of that flight of stairs Barry pushed me along the spacious landing, from which I could again see the front door.

Then I was hustled up a narrow staircase which had a window overlooking the street. I faltered on the step, wondering if there was any way I could smash that window.

'Don't even think it!' Barry drawled, giving me a nudge up to the turn of the stairs. The street was now behind me. He opened the door on the top landing. It was gloomy inside. Such light as there was came from a small and very dirty skylight.

He reached for the light switch. The single bulb suspended in the centre of the room gave out a dim glow. He opened another door which I hoped might lead into something a little less sepulchral, with a window perhaps. Loo, and washbasin. No window.

I looked around my cell. One camp-bed with pillow and duvet, and, in a corner, what looked like an old refrigerator.

'Water, and basic food,' Barry said.

'So – does that mean that you were expecting company?'

'Just a precaution,' he said. 'There's enough food for the best part of a week . . . if you manage it carefully.'

'And what will you be doing?'

His only reply was a wave of his hand. 'Goodbye Emma . . . Mrs Robson,' he said. 'Pity about the hair.'

He closed the door behind him and I heard the key grate in the lock.

Chapter 16

Any display of histrionics would have left Barry coldly unaffected. I was angry with myself for timing my visit without enough concern for the possible complications. With the operation at a critical stage every single moment counted, but to walk into this hole, like a lamb to the slaughter, was sheer idiocy. Or, was it? Henry knew where I was going. If I disappeared, he wouldn't need to raid the place to prove that Barry was definitely not on the side of the angels.

Barry had always been aloof – a loner – and on the rare occasions when our paths crossed, his lofty disdain for the rest of humanity made me wonder if he had any friends at all. He seemed a strange partner for Jessica, and was almost certainly responsible for the change in her personality over the years. I remembered her kittenish *joie de vivre* and her ability to transform any meeting of friends into a party, sadly now replaced by a thirst for gossip, and a grasping need for valuable possessions . . . at whatever cost. Her lack of concern for Harriet had sickened me.

Now, Barry appeared to be up to his neck in this mean scam, but quite how, I couldn't fathom. And where did Ian fit in?

Perhaps Barry, seeing Ian in plain clothes and with his own car, had not recognized him as the local Detective Inspector, and had approached him to find out why he was parked in Harriet's drive.

But that didn't really hold water. Barry would hardly want to draw attention to himself. Anyone connected with that scam would have been well briefed, and highly unlikely to voluntarily approach the opposition without good cause. But, *was* Ian the opposition?

Although I was fighting against it, I was unable to dismiss the concept that Ian could be the informer who was making nonsense of the team's efforts. I needed to find a plausible escape from this theory.

And what was Peter up to?

I was surrounded by people, each one of whom might be able to provide the information which would tie up the loose ends and close this miserable episode, but here I was, locked up in a little room, helpless, unable to do a thing about it.

If only I had brought my mobile phone I could have contacted Henry or Maxwell, told them what was going on. I'd been in too much of a hurry to get out of the flat before Ian returned.

Listening with my ear close to the door, I could hear no sounds in the house, and I wondered if Barry and Jessica had gone out. The door was solid. I tried poking the keyhole with a hairpin, and discovered that the key had been left in the lock. It was then that I noticed the gap under the door. If I could dislodge the key, it would fall on the landing floor. I had to find a method of retrieving it. It would have to land on something manoeuvrable, so that I could pull it back into the room. I sat on the folding bed and removed the pillow-case. If I could slide that under the door and get the key to drop onto it, I might be able to escape.

I spent some time winding hairpins together in an effort to make a primitive tool. I should have tried the pillow-case first. I could see nothing I could use to poke it through the narrow gap at the bottom of the door. I needed maximum coverage. There was no knowing where the key would drop.

The room was dusty, and my throat was dry, so I opened the

fridge and took a swig of chilled water, thankful for that, at least.

I was beginning to close the door when it dawned on me that one of the shelves might fit into the pillow-case and give me at least a fifty-fifty chance of capturing the key.

The pillow-case was too narrow. I solved the problem by using a hairpin to attack the stitching. Wonderful things, hairpins! Once I had undone a small section of the seam, I was able to rip the rest quite easily.

Carefully, with the fridge shelf to give it body, I coaxed the key trap underneath the door, but my plaited hairpins were no match for the stubborn key which refused to budge.

One of the stairs creaked, and I froze. The key was turning in the lock, and the door opened.

I had expected to see Barry, but it was Jessica.

'You'd better go . . . now,' she said. 'And leave this lot where it is.' She extracted the key and put it into the other side of the lock. 'Barry can think you got out on your own. There's no time to waste. I don't think he'll be out for long. He's taken the dog for a run in the park. Whatever made you mess up your hair like that? You'll need your hat. I've put it on the hall table.' She didn't appear to have connected me with Mrs Robson.

'Jessica, are you involved in this?'

She turned away. 'I'm going down to the kitchen now. Go out by the side-door.'

She was well ahead of me, and I heard the kitchen door slam as I reached the hall. I twisted my hair into a knot and stuffed it under the cotton hat, making my exit at speed.

Thick cloud had darkened the sky, and I didn't know what to do. I had no money, no credit cards. If I went to the police station I could get a message to Henry, but that would be a clear signal that I didn't trust Ian. I couldn't just stand there dithering. There was rain threatening. Barry could be back at any time. I had no choice.

I kept clear of the park. I knew the layout of the town well enough to use the shortest route through the streets to the police station. The young policeman who had allowed my car to be taken away was on duty at the desk.

'Dr Warwick?' he queried, frowning, as though not quite believing what he was seeing.

'I need to speak to Detective Superintendent Henry Abbot at Martinsfield . . . urgently!' He hesitated. 'Now!' I said, wondering if Ian had been right in thinking that the lad was not up to the job.

The duty sergeant came though to the desk.

'Dr Warwick! You look all in. Come through.' He lifted the hinged counter. 'The guvnor's not here at the moment. Shall I see if I can get hold of him? He's probably at his flat.'

'It's Detective Superintendent Abbot I need to speak to . . . at Martinsfield. It's very urgent . . . and confidential.'

'Right . . . you'd better use the guvnor's office.' He opened the door and ushered me inside. 'Use the phone on the left side of the desk. It . . . er. . . doesn't go through the switchboard.'

'And that matters?' I said.

'I reckon it does. Information is leaking from somewhere. I won't stand for it on my patch. I'm afraid I'll have to stay. I've already overstepped the mark allowing you in here.'

Remembering the number, I started to dial.

After I gave him swift details of my enforced stay at the Hammond house, Henry was all ears.

'And you say Mrs Hammond set you free?'

'Yes.'

'And it was clear that the husband had seen through the disguise earlier at the yard?'

'It looks that way, but someone may have warned him that something of the sort might happen, and he just played me along.'

151

'What are you going to do now? Will you go back to Ian's place?'

'D'you think I should?'

'Well, you must be in need of a relaxing bath and a good night's sleep. You've let Ian know what's been going on?'

'Not yet.'

'Emma . . . what's wrong? You can't imagine that Ian . . .' His voice faltered for a moment, and when he continued it was in a much tougher tone. 'Well . . . thank you for your confidence in me. I would never have put you down as stupid. Do you really imagine that I'd push you into the lions' den?'

'I wouldn't put it past you. Did you imagine I'd be safe visiting Jessica?'

'You know I don't like you taking unnecessary risks. But I'll admit I was hoping that you might be able to confirm that we were moving in the right direction. We're nearly there, but there are still one or two loose ends. I'll pick you up from Ian's flat tomorrow. About eleven?'

'*Please.* And can my hair be restored to some sort of normality? I feel like an old hag.'

'Of course. And ring Ian now and get back to his place. You'll be perfectly safe, I promise you.'

I put the phone down.

'Thank you, Sergeant . . .' I couldn't think of his name.

'Bowman, ma'am,' he said. 'Terry Bowman. Shall I ring the guvnor now?'

'I suppose you got the gist of the conversation?' I said.

He nodded. 'You can trust the guvnor, ma'am. But you're right to be cautious. There's someone around here who's as bent as the u-bend under the sink. Watch yourself, that's all I'll say.'

'I'd be glad if you'd ring him,' I said.

He was reaching for the phone when the door opened. It was the young constable who was at the front desk when I arrived.

'I'm off duty now, Sarge. I wondered if Dr Warwick would like a lift.'

'That'll speed things up a bit. Great idea, Colin.' Sergeant Bowman turned to me. 'I'll ring the guvnor and let him know you're on your way.'

'Thank you for the offer of a lift, Colin,' I said.

'After what happened to your car, I owe you one.'

I knew I looked a mess. I'd have taken a lift in a dustcart but, to my surprise, Colin drove up to the door in a snappy open sports car. It looked new. He could never have afforded that on his pay. A present from indulgent parents? A present to their dim son, if his bump of direction was anything to go by.

'You're going the wrong way,' I said, not wanting to do the scenic route – not even to let him show off his new toy. 'You'll have to circle the roundabout and start again.'

He put his foot down and the car shot forward.

'We're going for a little ride.' He had to shout above the noise of the engine. 'And they won't see me again in uniform.'

'Stop the car!' I was shouting too. 'I can't think what your parents were doing letting you loose in a deathtrap like this.'

'Nothing to do with them.' He laughed. 'Yeah! A deathtrap. I like it!' There was no humour in his laughter. 'It's going to be a nice little earner. And, I tell you, there's more goodies where this came from. I've had playing the dim young constable. It's the good life for me from now on.'

He took the slip road down to the motorway, and weaved his way through to the outer lane. Terrified, I clutched the door and the seat. The slipstream lifted my hat and my frantic grab missed it by inches. My hair streamed out behind me.

The road took a wide curve to the right.

'Get your bloody hair out of my eyes!' Colin yelled.

The car swerved across the lanes, narrowly missing disaster. There was an exit coming up, and he was again weaving between

the lorries and cars, reaching the exit with the clear aim of proving some sort of superiority.

There was a snarl-up ahead. We were hemmed in on all sides
and I was the target of a lot of the ribald remarks. I waited for
Colin to get into an argument with one of the lorry drivers. I
didn't have to wait long. Ignoring the whistles and catcalls, I was
out of the car, behind the lorry to our left, and up the grassy bank
towards the flashing lights of the police cars holding up the traffic.

I expected to find myself fighting to get them to ring and
confirm my story, but the sergeant who approached me said, 'Dr
Warwick?'

I could have kissed him, but, looking like a grubby old witch, I
simply pleaded to be allowed to sit in the back of one of the cars.
But then, I had a very unpleasant thought.

'Sergeant! D'you think you could isolate that sports car?'

He looked puzzled. 'It's not going anywhere,' he said. 'Both
ends of the slip road are blocked off.'

'But, I'm afraid it may blow up at any minute,' I said. 'Don't
take my word for it. Check with whoever sent you here. But don't
waste any time. There's probably an incendiary device tucked
away out of sight. A radio signal sets it off.'

My warning was taken seriously. Things began to move.
Vehicles on the lower slope were reversed on to the motorway, the
inside lane of which had already been cordoned off. The remaining lorries and cars were sent up to the roundabout with orders
to disperse without delay. This left one shiny red sports car
isolated in the middle of the road . . . minus its driver.

'Where is he? Where's Colin?' I said.

'He'll be taken care of, believe me,' the sergeant said. 'We
don't take kindly to members of the force who go off the rails.'

'Have you checked . . .' My words were swallowed up by the
explosion which blasted the small car, leaving behind a fiercely

burning tangle of metal and rubber which a waiting fire crew dealt with swiftly.

I learnt a few new words as the sergeant got over the shock.

'You . . . you knew! How could you be so sure?' he said, with more than a smattering of mistrust.

'Previous experience.'

He was looking at my hair with distaste.

'It is grim, isn't it?' I said.

'Er . . . sorry. I didn't mean to stare.'

There were approaching footsteps behind me. I turned and saw Ian coming towards me.

'I'm here to take you back to Martinsfield,' he said stiffly, and turned to the sergeant. 'Well done. I hear you were assigned to look after Dr Warwick.'

'If it wasn't for her, there would have been a bloody massacre on this road,' the sergeant said. 'Her warning convinced the guv'nor that it was worth the effort of clearing the area. God, if we hadn't got everything out of the way, we'd have had a casualty list as long as your arm.' He turned to me. 'Thanks Dr Warwick. Er . . . I don't know what you've done to your hair, but get it back to normal before the press get at you.'

'Thank you, sergeant,' Ian said stiffly. 'That will be all.'

'Sir.' The sergeant sprang to attention, recognizing a warning when he heard one.

'Thank you for looking after me,' I called after him, and turning back to Ian, I asked, 'Has it been a complete shambles?'

'Not entirely, but it's not over yet.'

'You were right about Colin,' I said. 'I thought he was a pleasant young man, but without much experience. I felt sorry for him.' I ran my fingers through my hair. 'I lost my hat in the mad race down the motorway. What will happen to him now?'

'He'll get what he deserves, but at least he won't be fried in his car.'

'You know . . . that I wasn't sure about *you*?' I said hesitantly, unable to meet his eyes.

'Yes. Are you willing to come with me now? Other arrangements can be made if you would rather not.'

'Look,' I said, awkwardly. 'I was so confused by this meeting you had with Barry.'

'What meeting with Barry? Barry who?'

'Barry Hammond. Jessica's husband. And don't play games with me. You were seen talking to him outside Harriet's house.'

'Who told you that?'

'The old girl at the café.'

'You didn't mention that earlier,' he said icily.

'It gave me a bit of a shock. I wanted . . . to think about it.'

He frowned. 'The only person I can remember talking to there, is the man who has taken on the yard down near the station.'

'That was Barry Hammond,' I said. 'He doesn't look a bit like the old Barry: dyed hair, and a face-job. But, you can't have known him very well, otherwise you'd have recognized the voice.'

'Are you sure about this?'

'Didn't Henry fill you in?'

'He told me about your confrontation in the yard.'

'From there, I went back to your flat and changed into my own clothes, and went to call on Jessica, but Barry arrived and locked me in their attic. He went out later and Jessica allowed me to escape.'

'Whatever made you go there in the first place?' he said.

'Henry thought it was worth the risk.'

'You trusted Henry, then?' he said.

'I had to let someone know what I was intending to do.'

'Well, Maxwell and Kate are expecting you. I've borrowed Sergeant Bowman's car. Less conspicuous than mine. It was his idea. Or, would you prefer to go with someone else?'

'Please, Ian, don't be so touchy. It was a hell of a situation to find myself in.'

'And how do you think I feel?'

'Can't you see how confusing it was?'

'You couldn't even give me the benefit of the doubt. That would be too much to ask, I suppose. Now, do you want me to take you to Martinsfield, or shall I find another driver?'

'If you go on like this, I'll bloody well walk!'

Chapter 17

Neither of us spoke on our way to the car. Not surprisingly, Ian was hurt by my inability to trust him without question, and I was frustrated that my effort to uncover more of the framework of the organization had backfired.

Ian drove half-way around the junction to join the motorway. The traffic was not so heavy now, most of it overtaking us, but one dark saloon was sticking doggedly to our tail.

Ian handed me his mobile phone.

'Try Henry's number. Ask him if we have an escort.'

I got through at once, and what I heard made me chuckle.

'It *is* Henry,' I said. 'He's going to be with us until we get back to Martinsfield.'

'Am I not to be trusted to get you back there on my own?'

Henry had not rung off. 'Tell him not to be a stupid bastard! he bellowed in my ear. 'There's too much at stake. I don't want to lose either of you.' The line went dead.

'Did you hear that last bit?' I said.

Ian grunted. I thought he was still angry, until his hand came over and squeezed mine. He put his foot down a little harder on the accelerator, and Henry remained a safe distance behind.

'Colin must have been given instructions, and what if he got through to his contact before he was arrested?' I said. 'They may well keep an eye open for us on the motorway.'

'Why d'you suppose Henry's on our tail?' Ian said soberly, and he kept glancing in the rear mirror. 'We've been caught on the hop too often. I should have trusted my gut feeling. And that young man should have realized that there was a limit to his usefulness, and no future once that had been used up. At least the little louse won't be about for some time.'

'And I felt sorry for him!' I said. 'I could kick myself.'

'You have to admit it, he played his part well. He should be grateful to you. He could have been sitting at the wheel when his car ignited.' Ian kept looking in the rear mirror. 'Keep your eyes open. We're going off at the next exit.'

'No. It's the one after that for Martinsfield.'

'Not if I read Henry's signal correctly.'

I turned my head. Henry was signalling to go left. Ian did likewise, and Henry caught up with us near the top of the slip road.

Overtaking, he guided us to the third exit and into a hypermarket car-park. He parked his car in front of ours and came towards us unfolding a map, as though seeking help.

'This car will be delivered to its owner first thing in the morning,' he said.

'By *me*,' Ian said emphatically. 'I want to see that Emma is safely back at Martinsfield House tonight.'

Without turning his head, Henry held up the map and said, 'Emma, you wouldn't want the lives of Maxwell and Kate and Madame Lambert to be jeopardized by your arrival, would you?'

'Of course not.'

'That is exactly what will happen if you return to the house tonight. You've both got to be part of a crowd of rowdies making a night of it. There are three motorized caravans on their way now. You may not believe it when you see them, but not one of the occupants has had any alcohol. They'll be all around your car, and you'll be changing places with two of them. And there's one more thing. Emma, can you get your hair up, fairly tightly around your head? I want you to wear this.' From under the map he produced a neat little wig, dark brown, quite near my own natural colour. 'Mrs Graham found this for me, and she thought these might be useful.' He added a hair-net and a bundle of hairpins. 'Put your hair up as soon as I'm out of the way, but don't do anything about the wig until the mob arrive and you've got a bit more cover. You may be glad to know that there is a change of clothes waiting for you in one of the caravans.'

'Someone really has thought this one through,' I said. 'You, Henry?'

'No. This exercise is controlled from the top, they've had this team lined up for days, but, at the last minute, I did suggest the change of clothes.'

'And bless you for that. How will we know which van to go for?'

'Don't worry, that's all been worked out.' He turned his attention to Ian. 'The idea is that you object to this rowdy crowd surrounding your car, and you get out of the car to protest. This is when Emma puts on the wig. Someone will open her door, and, under cover of the crowd, one of the women will take Emma's place.' He looked across at me. 'OK so far?'

I nodded, but I hadn't swallowed Henry's story about avoiding trouble at Martinsfield House. Things were hotting up and, for some reason, it was necessary for me to be part of the action.

'There'll be a light-hearted scuffle,' Henry said. 'This is when the other changeover will take place. One of the men will get into the car, ready to drive off. The departing car will be cheered on its way, and the two of you become part of the crowd and act as though you're having one hell of a time.'

'And where do we go from there?' I said.

'With a bit of luck, by that time the hypermarket manager will have phoned the police, and then it should be plain sailing. After the drivers have been breathalysed – you'll all be sent on your way.

'Where to?' I asked.

'To join other revellers in a field, sufficiently out of the way to avoid even the remotest connection with Martinsfield.'

'If the leak of information has now been plugged, let's hope it stays that way,' I said.

'Good luck,' Henry said. 'In case any unwelcome visitors arrive in the wake of our noisy friends, I'm now going to avoid any obvious connection with you or the caravan crowd. I can wheel my trolley, stock up for a month, and save myself the joys of getting tangled with pushchairs and howling kids.' He moved his car to distance himself from us, collected a trolley, and made his way towards the brightly lit entrance.

As instructed, I screwed my hair into a flat bun-like tangle, fixing it very firmly in place with the hairpins.

The number of people shopping so late at night surprised me, as did the motor caravans which were arriving, decked with balloons and paper streamers. The caravan crowd surrounded us, lolling against the car, and chanting bawdy songs.

Ian sounded the horn, as though wanting to move on, and getting no response he got out, shaking his fist. They mobbed him. In the tangle, one of the men got into the driver's seat.

'OK,' he said. 'Move!'

Things were not going according to plan. I should have left the car before this man arrived. I ducked down and put on the wig.

'Great!' he said. 'Even the DI won't know you. Now, get lost!'

My door was opened. A woman of similar build took my place, and I was swallowed up in the crowd, joining in with the well-planned romp.

'You look great!' Ian said, catching up with me. 'But, I think your wig is on back-to-front!' He was grinning broadly. 'Don't try to do anything about it. It goes with the drunken brawl.'

'Here come the cavalry,' I said, as two police cars arrived.

'Well briefed, I hope,' Ian said.

It was a pantomime, and it was some time before we all piled into the vans and were sent on our way.

The bawdy songs continued until we were out of ear-shot of the visitors to the hypermarket, and until it was certain that no one was tailing us. It was then that an embarrassed silence overtook us all. We were not now on the motorway, and I could not make out in which direction we were heading.

Ian and I were at the back of the caravan, and Ian was watching everything on the road, but he didn't allow me to get close to the window.

One of the caravans had gone on ahead of us, and the third was some distance behind. It was a dark night and there was little to see. The road took a winding course through the countryside, and we had been going along at a steady speed for about fifteen minutes when Ian said, 'That car's been behind us for the last couple of miles. I'm going up front to have a word with the driver.' Half-way there, he turned and said, 'How about a song? If we are being tailed, we still need to look and sound like a rowdy outing.'

One of them picked up his guitar, and we all began to sing – it was better than sitting waiting for something to happen.

Three of the men were sitting on the seat by the back window, swallowing what looked like beer, and trying to convince themselves and anyone who might be watching, that they were having a great time.

'That bugger's ignored umpteen safe passing-places,' one of them said. 'He's sticking to us like a lump of chewing gum.' He lifted his glass. 'And, I tell you, if I've got to drink much more of this muck we're going to have to stop so that I can have a pee.'

I wished he hadn't mentioned that. I too hoped fervently that we would soon reach our destination.

Calamity was avoided when the driver turned in to the car-park of an all-night diner. There were only two lorries there before us, and the stampede that followed when the brakes were applied reinforced the image of a boozy crowd having over-indulged on a night out. The car that had had been behind us had continued on its journey, or so we thought, but it was wait-ing for us in a lay-by near the next junction. The singing was more subdued now.

Our driver pulled in behind the car and got out.

'What's your game?' he said, and the singing stopped.

'I'm sorry if I've inconvenienced you, but I was taking advan-tage of your good steady driving to get home safely. I was called out to see one of my parishioners. I don't like driving at night. At my age, one does not see with the same clarity as in one's younger days.' The voice was measured and precise. 'Got far to go?' the driver said.

'Straight across the junction, and the rectory is on the left, next to the church. I shall not need to trouble you any further. Good-night to you.'

'G'night, Rev.'

We pulled out in front of the clergyman's car, and he was with us again, sticking like a leech. Our route ran straight across the roundabout and we saw the church tower silhouetted against the sky.

Still singing, we passed the overgrown hedges at either side of the entrance to the rectory, watching the small car behind us as it turned in to the drive.

A quarter of an hour later we drove into a field full of tents and caravans, and old cars.

'Your lot are parking over there,' the organizer of the gig said, pointing to one of our vans. 'Easier for you to get away in the morning. One more to come. Yes?'

'Should be here any time now,' our driver said, and began manoeuvring the van into position.

With the task completed, the revellers piled out, ready for an all-night session.

'Now that we're on our own,' Ian said. 'I think I should have a word with Henry. He'll be up to date with what's going on.'

He got through at once.

'Henry! We've arrived at the gig. Whoever is giving the orders certainly knows how to dish out the punishment. You weren't doing Emma any favours, transferring her to one of the caravans. She'd have been safely back at Martinsfield House by now. What's going on, Henry?' There was a pause. 'No. No trouble on the way. We thought we were being tailed towards the end of the journey, but it turned out to be the local vicar needing a light to lead him home.' There was a longer pause this time. 'Yes, that was the church,' Ian said. 'And the third van hasn't arrived yet.'

Henry was obviously saying something which alarmed Ian.

'Is there any possibility of a mistake? Might it have been a different church?' He groaned at the response. 'Oh hell! . . . Right, Henry. We'll wait for your call.'

'So, we *were* being tailed?' I said.

He nodded. 'That church is derelict. The rectory too. Can you get hold of our driver? I need to be here, out of sight and where no one else can hear what is being said, when Henry's call comes through. If we can match the description of this bogus clergyman with anyone already known to be involved, it would be one step forward. Be quick. We may need to move at a moment's notice.'

I found our driver chatting to the driver of the other van. He swore copiously when I told him why Ian wanted to see him, but he came fast enough.

'I should have smelt a rat the moment I put my head near his car window,' he said. 'His aftershave would have knocked out any normal congregation.'

'His eyes?' I said. 'What about his eyes?'

He frowned. 'You couldn't have seen his eyes from where you were. How did you know. . . ?'

'Answer the question,' Ian said. 'His eyes?'

'I was surprised by those, I'll admit,' he said. 'They were really bright . . . bright blue . . . gave me the creeps.'

'Harriet's attacker!' I said.

Ian nodded, and turned to the driver. 'This could be it.'

'Shall I tell the guvnor?'

'Find him and tell him he's needed here.'

The call was already through to Henry. As the driver closed the door, I heard Ian say, 'Right. Emma and I stay put until you tell us otherwise, and Mark is in charge of this end of the operation? Is that what we're all supposed to call him . . . Mark? And what about the third van?' From the expression on his face I could see that it was not the best news of the day. 'Any casualties?' His face relaxed as he listened. 'Thank God for that! Yes. We'll wait for further instructions.'

'What happened to the other van?' I said.

'It was forced off the road and down an embankment. The drivers for this exercise were hand-picked. Just as well. He kept the van upright. A few minor injuries. Nothing serious. They will be joining up with the other van, which will soon be on the move.'

'And we have to twiddle our thumbs here while the motivator behind all of this is probably sitting somewhere not too far away, laughing his or her head off.'

'You think the creature at the head of this mob could be female?' Ian raised an eyebrow.

'Not beyond the bounds of possibility,' I said. 'But I doubt it.'

'You don't think our clergyman is the top dog?'

'I've been wondering about that.'

'Nothing more definite than that? What does your intuition tell you?'

'You have a hunch, but I have intuition, is that what you think?'

'*Touché!*' he said, and grinned.

The man who arrived at the door looking like a tough, scruffy drunk, was responsible for this part of the operation and, from his bearing when out of the public eye, I gathered that he was well up in the pecking order.

'Dr Warwick, if you wouldn't mind going into the other van while we discuss the present position . . .' He clearly wanted me out of the way.

'I could do with a breath of air,' I said, coldly, feeling a bit miffed.

The gig was still filling the night with the efforts of several groups with drums, and with guitars which might have had only one string apiece judging from the monotonous beat. There were two fires burning, and the smell of smoke and charred food drifted on the light breeze.

I suddenly realized that I was hungry.

The two drivers were leaning against their vans, keeping an eye on things.

'Been thrown out while they have a powwow, have you?' one of them said. 'Never mind, love. Don't look so worried. We know what we're up against, but we're reasonably safe here. And there's some grub on the way.'

Through the milling throng came familiar faces, and a pile of beefburgers. Not my usual fodder, but, just what I needed right then. The smell of the onions permeated the air, and I accepted my portion with enthusiasm.

We sat around, like all the others, looking completely relaxed, and as though we were having a great time. Mark and Ian had not been overlooked. Their share of the food had been delivered. This team had been well drilled.

But, where was Mr Smith, I wondered. Was he perhaps still wearing a clerical collar? I was probably the only one who would recognize him, and he must know that only too well.

Chapter 18

Smith dominated my thoughts. Were he and Harriet's attacker one man with two disguises? And what was going on at that derelict rectory? Where did Barry fit in? The big chief, or, simply the manager of the yard, and neither the owner nor the tenant? I knew that he loved his children, and tolerated his wife's attitude to life, but could he be so contemptible, so full of his own importance, that he was willing to risk everything for a tainted reward?

'Snap out of it! You look as though you're at a wake.' Our driver was laughing as though I had said something hilarious. 'Don't look now, but there's a guy beside that red-and-green tent who's had his eye on you just a bit too long for comfort. He's not one of ours. I think I need to let the guvnor know.' He slapped me on the back and I laughed and pushed him away. He half-turned, exchanging a bit of banter with several of the men who were swilling back some of the innocent brew. There must have been a danger signal exchanged, because they crowded around like a group of happy drunks, blocking the view with strings of balloons, and giving the driver a chance to get into the van, unseen.

One of the men had a Polaroid camera, and we all posed with enthusiasm, moving at the wrong moment, and making it necessary to repeat the process several times, hopefully, getting a

picture of the watcher in the background. The results were taken
to Mark.

I tried not to look directly at the red-and-green tent, but now
the others were waving in that direction. I waved too, but there
was no one there who even remotely jogged my memory. Probably
a false alarm. The whole operation seemed to consist of one step
forward, and two steps back.

I was trying to make it look as though this was my idea of a good
night out, but my concentration kept slipping a cog to Smith. If
the man who had attacked Harriet was also our bogus clergyman,
there was no reason why he should be on his own at the rectory.
It was also an ideal spot for storing stolen antiques until the costly
police exercise had been called off, as it surely would be if there
were no signs of further progress. However, it seemed increasingly
evident that it was not only the police who were involved in these
investigations.

There had seldom been a more worthy cause for united effort:
to see justice done, and to know that at least some of the victims
would be recompensed for their losses. But time was running out.

Harriet's strange connection with this piece of history had
been my initial concern, and to see her back in her own house,
with her own things around her, was high on my list of priorities.
The consequent trashing of my apartment and car, plus a selfish
need to get back to my current project without further complications, had persuaded me that my continued involvement with the
investigations made sense. I had the impression that for the hard-
bitten types who formed the core of the team, some of them from
the USA, this had become a campaign on behalf of those people
who had been robbed of homes, of freedom, and of life itself.

I saw the door of our caravan opening and closing again. It was
impossible to see who was going in, or coming out, but a man was
forcing his way through the crowd. Reaching me, he took me a
few steps away from the others, and said urgently, 'Mark wants to

see you right away. I'll let this lot know where you've gone.'

There were curtains over the caravan windows. I was prepared to find both men waiting for me, but there was no sign of Ian.

'Come in, and shut the door,' a terse voice said, adding, 'er . . . please. Do sit down. I have a request to make. Please feel free to refuse. I mean that. I don't want you to feel under any obligation.'

'Where's Ian?' I said, looking around the caravan, but it seemed that we were the only occupants.

'He's gone back to the place where the phoney rector was dropped off. We need to discover if that is where the whole organization is concentrated, or if it's just a collection of petty crooks, hired for a one-off bluff to sniff us out. Half of the team will be in position by now, ready to pull them all in. However, if we make the mistake of being fooled with a load of small fry, we'll have blown our cover – and lost the big fish into the bargain. That would negate everything we have worked to achieve. Our difficulty is that you are the one most likely to recognize Smith, the man we now have good reason to believe is at the centre.'

'You seem more convinced of his role than I am,' I said.

'We've had help from our counterparts in Germany.'

I suppose I looked surprised.

'Oh, yes! They want to see an end to this just as much as we do. We sent them copies of the photographs that Edward and Harriet Travers took when they found what was left of the house belonging to the antiques dealers. They made enquiries locally, and discovered that one of the men was a Hans Schmidt who had worked for the owners of the house in the thirties. They turned up the old files and found out that before the war he'd been in trouble with the police more than once. It was thought that in late forties or early fifties he had settled in the USA.'

'Schmidt . . . Smith. If he had a criminal record, he'd surely have changed his name completely, not simply translated it,' I said.

'Smith is one of the most common names in New York City,' he said blandly. 'If he wanted anonymity he couldn't have done better. We have some colleagues from the USA on the team.' He looked at his watch. 'Right. I agreed to give Mr Foster a twenty-minute start to locate the best spots to see without being seen.'

'Then, you hadn't counted on me refusing?'

'With *your* reputation . . .' He dismissed the idea. 'Now, get yourself to the exit. Most of the campers are staying overnight, but there are a number of them on their way home. It'll be relatively easy to get a lift. Another point. Ian is carrying a little gadget which will tell us to move in. If this electronic wonder fails – for any reason – you'll have to find a way to alert us . . . any sort of noise will do, but it'll have to be loud enough to be heard by the men who will be in position beyond the boundaries of the church-yard. It is vital that we get a positive confirmation before we break cover. Good luck, Emma.'

'Thank you, Mark. I think I'm going to need it.'

If someone was watching me, I didn't want to make my departure too obvious. Some campers were leaving. I made as though to go towards the loo but, backtracking, I hurried to the exit, my thumb in the direction of the rectory.

The first car passed by, but the second stopped and I asked to be dropped at the roundabout near the old church.

'Sure, love.' The driver knew where I wanted to go. It was the only roundabout for miles. 'Great gig, wasn't it?'

The car was packed, and I was manhandled into the back seat for a fifteen-minute drive of excruciating discomfort.

'Thanks a lot,' I said, squeezing out of the sardine can.

They were a happy, friendly car-load. I felt wretched as they continued their journey, turning off the roundabout, and out of sight.

Everything was deathly quiet. Crossing the road, my sandals making no sound, I felt like a lost ghost. There was gravel on the drive so I stepped into the shrubbery, equally overgrown and a perfect place to hide.

A movement on the gravel made me freeze.

I held my breath.

'Emma?'

'Ian?' The whisper had scarcely passed my lips when a hand was clapped over my mouth. I bit it . . . *hard*!

'Dammit, Emma. Save your venom for the enemy!'

'Sorry . . . for a moment I thought you *were* the enemy. Did I do any damage?' My voice was almost inaudible.

'I'll live. When we get nearer the house, not a whisper unless it's vital. I've found a place where you can see the main room where they all seem to be . . . including Hammond.'

I wasn't expecting that bit of news. If this operation turned out to be a success, it looked as though Barry might not be around to see his children growing up.

'Have you seen anyone who might be Smith?' I asked, keeping my voice as low as I could. 'Why do you need me? You'd surely remember his face from the mug shot.'

'You've seen him standing next to you. There's a great difference between that and a mug shot.'

We were moving slowly through the shrubbery now, both concentrating on avoiding the assorted rubbish dumped near the edge of the drive.

A slamming door made us halt in our tracks. Two men were beginning to walk slowly along the drive, shining torches into the tangled borders at either side. Ian pointed to the ground, and we both gently lowered ourselves until we were on our knees behind piles of junk.

The men carried on to the end of the drive, where they watched as another crush of campers went by.

171

'I don't think much of this job,' one of them said. 'I'm quitting after tonight.'

'Don't let the boss hear you say that, or you'll find yourself having a nasty accident.'

'I'm not the only one who has had enough.'

'Well, you'd better leave on the quiet, and get away as far and as fast as you can. I'd come with you, but I need the loot.'

'I'm not going without the five hundred he promised us.'

'Don't push your luck. Tomorrow evening we'll all be at home with our feet up. Remember, he's promised us a good bonus. You don't want to miss out on that.'

Slowly, they came back up the drive, passing us again and going back into the house.

'Now we can get a bit closer,' Ian whispered. 'That's the window you need to watch. I'll have to leave you for a few minutes while I check the transport. We don't want them getting away before the party starts. When I come back, hopefully I'll be able to send the go-ahead signal on this little beauty.' He held a small gadget in his hand – something like the old-fashioned cigarette lighters. 'I won't be long.'

The window was shut, the glass mainly shattered. There were no curtains. Antique furniture of every description was being enclosed in protective padding, and transferred to large packing cases, and there was a trolley parked in the centre of the room where one of the packing cases was being manoeuvred into place. It looked as though the time had come for the final exit.

I saw Barry Hammond giving orders, and checking some sort of list on a clipboard he was holding. It was clear that he was not the big chief. And then Smith arrived on the scene. Not Smith, the senile ornithologist. The face now matched the hands for lack of ageing: firm features, and the hair without a wisp of grey. A man in his mid-forties at a guess.

Where was Ian? He could activate the gadget and the whole

house of cards would collapse.

As I watched, Smith was rubbing his eyes. I doubted that he would have done that with contact lenses in place. So, he could have three separate identities: the old man at the hotel, perhaps even using his father's passport; the bright-eyed brute who nearly killed Harriet; and the Smith I saw in front of me: eyes cold, and without mercy.

There were sounds of a fight and, to my horror, Ian was propelled into the room by the two men we had seen walking down the drive. We had watched them going back into the house, but they must have been sent out again to check other areas.

Ian was bleeding profusely from a head wound, and one of the men was holding the all-important gadget. Smith picked it up, removed the batteries and, in triumph, threw them across the room.

I took my chance to get nearer to the window, and trod very carefully across the gravel drive and into the shrub border edging the house. There had to be something I could do.

Smith was standing over Ian, and there was a gun in his hand aimed at Ian's head.

Using every scrap of strength I could muster, I picked up one of the stone slabs edging the border and flung it at the window. The effect was electrifying. Everyone, barring Smith, dived for cover.

'Get him out of here,' he shouted, grabbing Barry's arm. 'Take him up to the top of the tower. With the whole thing primed to go up in flames, we can't lose. They'll think twice before making a move.'

I ran to the back of the house and into the churchyard, hiding behind a large headstone. Three men, two of them carrying Ian, were already at the gate. They stopped at the church door, the two men refusing to go any further.

'The whole bloody lot could go up at any time. I'm off.'

'Me too.'

Barry stood there, watching them run off into the night, and then bent down and lifted Ian into his arms, but he didn't go into the church. He was walking in my direction. I didn't move a muscle. He stopped. I could have reached out to touch him.

'OK, Emma, I know you're there. Wait until that cloud goes over the moon, and then stick close behind me. No time to explain.'

We threaded our way to the far side of the graveyard, and Barry gently lowered Ian on to the ground. Something between a groan and a sigh told us that he was still alive.

'I've got to go back now,' he said.

'But, does this mean. . . ?'

'That I'm not the villain you thought I was? Let's just say that, if we both get through this, you say nothing about my part in it.' He sighed. 'I wish to God we could get the go-ahead through to our lot before it's too late.'

He was off like a moving shadow.

Tearing the sleeves off the shirt I was wearing, I ripped them into makeshift bandages for Ian's head, hoping this might help to stop the bleeding.

The clouds kept covering the moon. Ian's eyes opened momentarily and he said, 'We must let them know ... we must . . .' and he was gone again.

The church tower. Perhaps there were still bells up there. A couple of minutes would be enough.

I crossed the graveyard to the church. The bell tower was over the porch which was crammed with all manner of junk: fodder for the incendiary, I guessed.

Clambering up the uneven steps to the tower, I grabbed the only rope in view, a frayed remnant, and pulled several times. There was a clatter and something seemed to slip. In desperation and not a little fear, I tried again, and again, following what I had seen on television and in films. I had to make the bell stand on its head. That I seemed to remember. Then ... keep the rhythm, allowing the rope to move freely through my cupped hands as it went upwards. Not too far. Then down again. I could have cheered. The bell was doing its stuff. I only hoped that the team would recognize it for what it was.

I kept it going for two or three minutes, afraid to allow the rope too free an upward sweep. My hands were burning. I was making a mess of it, but the bell was making a splendid noise.

Enough. If our lot hadn't got the message by now, it would be a waste of time to go on. I needed to get back to Ian.

I ran down the stone steps, dodging the mounds of rubbish and the smashed wooden pews piled high at the head of the aisle and in the porch. In seconds, I was out of the door, making for the spot where Ian lay. He was unconscious. I felt for a pulse, but couldn't find one. My fingers had lost their sensitivity and only registered pain.

A whistle blew, and suddenly, so did the tower! The belching smoke and the leaping flames were almost like living creatures: horrifying in their ferocity. The heat was already reaching us, as was the sound of gunfire.

'I'm burning!' Ian groaned and opened his eyes. 'Emma ... Emma ...' he gasped, lapsing again into unconsciousness.

I tried to shield him from the heat, placing myself between Ian and the raging fire. There was nothing I could do now but wait for help to arrive.

At last, the noise abated. Floodlights illuminated the whole area. Out of the smoke, led by Barry, a stretcher party was coming at the double in our direction.

Chapter 19

Ian was in the ambulance. I wanted to go with him but there were others who needed more urgent medical attention.

'They got your message loud and clear,' Barry said, returning to me after having made sure that the ambulance driver had a smooth run out of the drive. A grin spread across his face. 'But, if you're looking for a job as a bellringer, forget it.' He touched the wig which still covered my dyed hair. 'What a crime. All in the line of duty, I suppose.'

'Is that it?' I said. 'Is it all over?'

'Not yet. There are still loose ends to be tied up. We've got to be sure that we have every available scrap of evidence. This case has got to be watertight. I'm off to the States tonight with my American counterpart, to nose out Smith senior.'

'In all the years I've known you, I never thought of you as . . .'

He put his fingers against my lips. 'Forget what you know. I'm just Barry Hammond . . . a guy with a rough tongue, and an overblown opinion of himself.'

'Does Jessica know what you do?'

'It may surprise you to know that she does.'

'But, she's never even hinted . . .' I was speechless.

'Jessica knows that we'd lose everything if she opened her

mouth. She's not stupid. A bit scatty at times maybe. And don't fool yourself, I know that she let you out of the attic room.'

'Does she know that?'

'No. I'll let her struggle with her conscience for a while.'

'Bastard!' I said and, although the expression on his face remained neutral, his eyes showed that he was anticipating the prospect with a certain relish. 'So . . .' I continued, angry, but reluctantly amused at the same time, 'am I to take it that you knew all along that there was no Mrs Robson . . . that it was me?'

He nodded. 'I knew what you'd been asked to do. And . . . by the way . . . you owe me thirty quid.'

I had to laugh.

'But, why lock me away if we are both on the same side?'

'For your safety . . . and mine. I'd worked hard to get myself accepted by the opposition. I couldn't risk things going wrong when we were almost ready for the final swoop.' He checked the time. 'I've got to get back home soon to change and get off to Heathrow.' He grabbed my hand. 'Come on. I'll drop you at the Martinsfield hospital. That's where Ian is being taken.' I couldn't stop myself crying out loud, as Barry held my hands up to the light.

'Good grief! Why didn't you show them to the medics?'

'Not exactly life-threatening,' I said.

'Well, I'm getting you to the hospital right now. You need to get those hands into cold water, and then they'll put on a light dressing.'

'You make me sound like a salad,' I said, trying to laugh.

'It's no joke. A bit longer tugging at the bell rope and you'd have been in real trouble.'

'A bit longer, and I wouldn't be here now,' I reminded him. 'But it was you who took the big risk when you saved Ian's life. If Smith had found out, he'd have killed you on the spot.'

'He was too busy attempting to get the show on the road.'

But we both knew exactly what Smith would have done.

'Ian . . . will recover?' I said, my confidence at a low ebb.

'He's tough.' No tender reassurance. Barry's voice was revert-ing to normal. 'Where the hell has my car gone?' The arrogance was showing, but I was afraid that it was a cover for his belief that Ian could be dying.

One of the caravan toughs was directing the departing vehicles. 'Hang on, sir,' he called over his shoulder. 'I know your car. I'll get one of the lads to take over here, and I'll find it.'

Barry and I perched on an old bench and waited.

'Any idea where Peter is?' I asked.

'Peter?' Barry said, with an inflexion in his voice which hinted that he had little regard for his brother-in-law.

'Just before you arrived on the scene last night, Jessica was telling me that Peter had gone on holiday the day after they had called at Martinsfield House.'

'That's right. He went off about the middle of last week, and the longer he stays away the better.'

'But, he's back,' I said. 'I saw him in the shopping arcade with Jessica, yesterday, looking for the stolen antiques.' And why hadn't Jessica wanted me to know he was back? I wondered.

'Jessica was with him?' Barry looked puzzled.

'Well . . . yes,' I said reluctantly, not wanting to land her in trou-ble again. 'As Mrs Robson, I was buying a cheap watch. In fact . . . Jessica paid for it.'

'What the hell made her do that?'

'She'd made a rather offensive remark a little earlier, and was showing her remorse.' I smiled, still relishing that moment.

'And she didn't recognize you?'

'No.'

'A watch from Jessica, and thirty quid from me . . . not bad, all considered. How do I explain that on my expenses? As for Peter, I'll sort him out. You can leave it to the professionals now. But, you'll still need to watch your step. The lout who attacked Harriet seems to have got through the net.'

'You've got Smith junior, haven't you?' I said.

'Oh, yes. We've got that black-hearted sod.'

'Look in his pockets for tinted contact lenses. That's where you'll find those brilliant-blue eyes.'

Barry looked unimpressed. 'Then tell me, on the night of the robbery, how did he get out of the hotel late in the evening without anyone wondering where he was going, and why?'

'He'd probably already made a habit of taking a late stroll,' I said. 'Keeping up the ornithologist pretence, studying the night-life of the owls. And, if the local paper is to be believed, there's at least one nightingale singing its head off in the woods near the Common. What better cover could he have had?'

Barry grinned, and thew up his hands in surrender. 'If you ever want to change your vocation . . .'

'Not on your life!'

I could see his car being parked further up the drive. Mark was standing nearby. Barry hailed him as we approached, and told him about my theory.

'Tinted contact lenses!' Mark exclaimed. 'No wonder he made a fuss. Without them, it would have been a hard job to prove that the two Smiths were, in fact, one. The lenses are with the odds and ends from his pockets – including one vicious handgun.'

'Which he was about to use on Ian when Emma threw a rock through the window, and sent most of them running for cover,' Barry said.

'Fortunate for Ian that she did. It would have damn near blown his head off.'

I could feel the world spinning and, completely humiliated, I was as sick as a dog.

'Get her into the car,' Mark said.

'I may be sick again,' I protested.

'Don't worry.' Barry opened the car door. 'The kids don't travel well, so I've always got a good supply of plastic bags.'

'In that case,' Mark said, 'use two of them to protect her hands. It will help to stop them getting dehydrated. Get her to hospital as fast as you can. I'll let them know you're coming. He took one of the bags and placed it over my left hand, and Barry dealt with the right hand.

We turned out of the drive to the muffled cheers of the caravan crowd. I was laughing and crying at the same time.

We had joined the motorway again when Barry said casually, 'You always hated my guts, didn't you?'

'I didn't hate you, Barry. I just didn't . . . *like* you. You didn't encourage friendship.'

'Perhaps now, you understand why?'

'Up to a point, but did you have to be so crushingly pompous and dismissive?'

There was a long pause, and I felt that I had been too blunt.

'Sorry, Barry,' I said. 'But, you did ask . . . and, if it's any consolation, you've done a magnificent job this time. If it weren't for you, Ian would be dead. I take it that *he* knew which side you were on, and what you were doing?'

'Only when it became obvious that he needed to know.'

'Needed to know,' I repeated. 'And, no doubt, sworn to secrecy.' Now, I could appreciate Ian's dilemma.

'That's right.'

'Perhaps too many people know now, or have guessed.' I was thinking aloud.

'Yes. When the mess is tidied up, I'll probably be put on the back-burner for a while.'

'With more time for the family?'

'Yes.' He said it with great satisfaction, adding in the same breath, 'Are those hands giving you a lot of pain?"

'Could be worse,' I said.

'Another five minutes and we'll be there. I'll have to leave you in casualty . . . running a bit short of time.' He re-checked his watch. 'Jessica knows I'm coming. She'll have a change of clothes ready, and my bag packed, so – allowing time for a shower and a quick shave – I can be in and out again in fifteen minutes.'

'Strange to think I never really knew you,' I said.

'We'll understand each other better in the future. But, in company, be warned, I'll treat you no differently than in the past.'

The car drew up outside the entrance to Casualty. The hospital had been warned ahead. A porter with a wheelchair was there waiting for me. I waved to Barry and the porter took me to one of the treatment rooms.

'Do you know how Mr Foster is?' I asked the nurse.

'The doctor's just coming. He'll be able to tell you,' she said, standing back as he swept into the small room.

'Did I hear you enquiring after Mr Foster?' he said, as the nurse removed the plastic bags from my hands. 'A nasty crack on the head. We'll know more in the morning.'

'Can I see him?'

'Tomorrow. It's you who needs attention at the moment.'

Sunlight was streaming in through the window, and I was emerging from a nightmare in which Smith was torching my apartment.

'Smith! It has to be Smith!' I cried out, cringing as I tried to use my hands to prop myself up in bed.

'Steady, Emma!' It was Maxwell's voice. He was standing by my bed, and Kate was helping me to settle back onto the pillows.

'It was so real,' I said. 'But it doesn't make sense . . . unless there are three generations: the original employee, his son, and his grandson. Miss Tucker, the one who let the arsonist into the building, said he was a young man.'

'You've done your share,' Maxwell said. 'Henry couldn't tell us much, but they're all very pleased with themselves. Without

Harriet's original suspicions, and your delving, this wouldn't have got off the ground. It's time for you to think of yourself for a change.'

The door opened and a nurse came in carrying a small and rather tatty bunch of flowers with a note attached.

'The porter says a caravan stopped outside, and a very scruffy man insisted that this was for you,' she said, slightly embarrassed.

Kate picked up the note and put it in front of me.

It read:

> From you know where, and you know who
> with our thanks and admiration
>
> The Drunken Mob

I started to laugh, and I'm afraid Kate and Maxwell and the nurse thought I was about to lapse into hysterics.

'Shall I take them away?' the nurse said, picking up the flowers and holding them at arm's length.

'No. Put them on my locker, please. I know it must be difficult to believe, but they are very precious to me.'

She shrugged her shoulders. 'If that's what you want.'

'Don't worry. I'll take them with me when I go,' I said.

'I've brought some clothes.' Kate pointed to a suitcase near the door. 'The doctor wants to see you, and he's fairly confident that you'll be able to come back with us this morning. If you feel well enough, Mrs Graham can come in this afternoon to deal with your hair and to give you a facial. That should be something of a tonic, don't you think?'

'Kate! You think of everything.'

'Now that I'm married to Maxwell, I can't help thinking of you as my daughter. You don't object, do you?' She looked worried, as though she had trespassed on forbidden territory.

'You will remember that I'm a very independent woman.'

'I'll try,' she said, and I hoped she meant it. 'I thought you'd want to know how Harriet is, so I rang the hospital this morning. She should be able to go home on Wednesday or Thursday.'

'I won't be much use to her by then,' I said.

'You're staying with us until those hands have healed.'

'But I promised Harriet that I'd be there when she was ready to come out of hospital.'

'My dear, you didn't know then that your hands would be in this state.'

I tried to convince Kate that Harriet and I would be able to manage, and that I needed to get on with my new project. The clients had been very patient, especially as I had been unable to tell them what had been going on.

'Get her to come down to Martinsfield for a week or two,' Kate said. 'Madame Lambert thrives on spoiling people.'

'I don't think Harriet would like to leave her house empty.'

'The house must have been empty while she's been in the hospital.'

'No, Ian arranged for one of the constables to sleep there, and a new security system is being installed. Harriet needs to get home to re-establish herself and, most of all, to get her confidence back.'

'I suppose you're right,' Kate said. 'Would you like me to take you over to see her tomorrow?' She looked towards the door. 'The doctor's coming. I'll come back when he's gone, and help you into your clothes.' It was said tentatively, and I wanted to hug her for making such an effort to leave me with my freedom unfettered.

Chapter 20

'How's Mr Foster?' were my first words as the doctor came into the room.

'He had a reasonably good night. No visitors until late this afternoon, I'm afraid.' He examined my hands and told me to come in the following day for fresh dressings.

I went back to Martinsfield with Maxwell and Kate and, in the early afternoon, Mrs Graham arrived to work her magic. Mrs Robson was banished, and Emma Warwick felt able to face the world again. Mrs Graham was going on to another appointment, to see a young woman whose face had been gashed in a street brawl.

'A remarkable woman,' Kate said, as we walked out on the terrace after seeing her off.

'I thought we'd be haunted by Mrs Robson for the rest of our lives,' Maxwell said. 'The woman's a genius!' He paused. 'Damn! I think that's the phone.' Reluctantly he got out of his chair, and came back a few moments later. 'Barry wants to speak to you, Emma . . . the study phone.'

I ran across the drawing-room and into the study, clumsily picking up the receiver.

'Hello Barry. Did you miss your flight?'

'No. I'm in New York. We've got him! Along with the other

184

organizers of this scam, Smith senior is in custody. He'd shifted most of the stuff to the UK, but he still had three pieces of furniture in his apartment, for which Harriet has photos and detailed provenance, proving that they were originally in the house owned by Michael and Klara.'

'Congratulations!'

'There's more,' he said solemnly. 'The records tell us that Michael, . . . Michael Fischer . . . was knocked down and badly injured in a road accident in May 1951.'

'Oh . . .' The triumph evaporated. 'Michael and Klara . . . are they still alive?'

'No contact as yet. Enquiries are continuing.'

'Anything known about our Mr Smith?' I said.

'A bit-part actor. That is, when he's not otherwise occupied.'

'That follows. Has he got a grown-up son, by any chance?'

'What makes you ask that?'

'When my flat was torched, Miss Tucker told the police that the man supposedly visiting his aunt, was young, and well-dressed, and with charming manners. The bird-watcher, and the man who attacked Harriet we now accept are one and the same. But also playing a fresh-faced young man? I doubt it. Can you find out if Smith senior has a grandson with a suitable degree for an arsonist, and a smooth tongue?'

'Interesting thought. I'll investigate.'

'Can Harriet now have her furniture and other valuables returned?' I said.

'As soon as possible, but there's bound to be some delay.'

'Thank you for the update,' I said.

'And . . . Emma . . . if you don't want to get involved in this sort of caper again, just keep a low profile for a while. OK?'

'I understand.' I paused. 'You haven't mentioned Peter.'

'You've got it in for him, haven't you?'

'One minute he seems like the old Peter, pleasant enough, but always fairly self-centred; and the next he folds up like an oyster under attack.'

'Stand-offish . . . like me?'

'Oh!' The answer stunned me, but I knew better than to ask any questions. 'You must be pleased that things have gone so well,' I continued, as though there had been no hiatus. 'I'll be seeing Harriet tomorrow. I suppose I can't tell her anything about your part in this?'

'Not even a hint. You can tell Harriet, and Maxwell and Kate, that you think things are going fairly well. And . . . tell Harriet you bumped into me, and I asked you to give her my love.'

The line went dead.

Fazed, I put the phone down. Was it possible that Harriet's open dislike of Barry could have been feigned . . . for his protection?

I went out to the hall where Maxwell and Kate were waiting for me, doing their best not to look as though they were itching to know what the call was about.

'Things are going well. It seems that certain people will get their comeuppance, and Harriet will be getting her stolen property returned,' I said. 'But that is for *your* ears only. I can also tell Harriet, of course, but no one else.'

I was not yet able to look back on the previous twenty-four hours with anything approaching *sang-froid*.

'Please . . . don't ask me to tell you anything about last night. Not now. It was a nightmare. I thought Ian was going to die.'

'We're so relieved to see you in one piece,' Maxwell cut in. 'Henry couldn't give us any details, but we gathered that you were involved in some sort of cleaning-up operation, and that it was not exactly a picnic. I take it that you were both in the thick of it when Ian was injured.'

'We're not going to talk about it any more,' Kate said firmly. 'Ian is lucky to be alive. The ward sister told me that, if the X-rays

186

are satisfactory, he may be transferred to his local cottage hospital tomorrow. Emma, please let us do what little we can to help. It is such a joy to have you back safe and, more or less, sound.'

We met Henry on our way in to the hospital. He was coming out.

'I'm glad to see that Mrs Graham has done the trick,' he said to me, after greeting us all. 'And I take it you accept now that Ian is to be trusted?'

'I'm ashamed I ever doubted it,' I said. 'But, Henry, you gave me one hell of a job, and you didn't fill me in on any of the details. Leading us in to that hypermarket car-park, letting me think you were making sure we'd be safe . . .' I stopped in full flow. 'Hell! I suppose Ian knew what that was all about too!'

'Er . . . well . . .'

I could see that he was searching for the right reply. 'Give it up, Henry,' I said. 'It was your problem. I must have been off my trolley to have anything to do with *any* of you.'

He opened his mouth.

'No!' I insisted. 'Not another word.' I paused, still hopping mad. 'I wouldn't have minded if you'd told me what was planned.'

'We'll nip in to see Ian for a few moments,' Maxwell said, tactful for once in his life.

When they were out of earshot, I asked Henry, 'D'you know anything about Peter Jackson?'

'Such as?'

'For starters, is he a part of this operation?'

'What makes you ask?'

'Don't keep hedging, Henry.'

'Then, tell me exactly what it is that is worrying you.'

'When all this started, Peter and Jessica seemed keen to get their aunt to move to a home for the elderly. They knew that all her valuable property would go to them eventually and, Peter in particular, seemed a bit too enthusiastic about the idea.'

187

'And you think he was part of the scam?'

'If he thought he could get away with it, without actually caus-
ing anyone any physical damage . . . just . . . maybe. He enjoys
extravagant living, and he's never been one for sticking to one job
for long.'

'Do you know where he is now?' Henry said.

'I saw him yesterday afternoon when, dressed as Mrs Robson, I
was in the shopping arcade. Jessica told me later that Peter was on
holiday, that he'd gone the day after they'd both been to
Martinsfield House. Nothing ties up.'

'He was in New York last week. He arrived back in the UK early
yesterday, and left again late last night . . . on the same flight that
Barry Hammond nearly bust a gut to catch.'

I opened my mouth, but he said, 'Peter's . . . useful. Don't ask
me any more questions. I've said too much already. Now, go and
see Ian before he thinks I'm making off with you. And don't think
I wouldn't, given half a chance.'

It was the first time I felt like chuckling.

I crossed the corridor to the partly open door of Ian's room.
Kate got up from her chair when she saw me and, dragging
Maxwell by the arm, she said, 'We'll see you in the car-park,
Emma. Don't stay too long. Ian looks tired, and so do you.'

I had the small bunch of wild flowers held awkwardly in one
hand, and the card in the other.

Ian put a hand up to touch my hair.

'I'll never forget the first time I saw Mrs Robson,' he said.

'Like . . . yesterday,' I reminded him.

'And what am I to make of these?' He touched the faded flowers.

'Read the card.'

A slow smile spread over his face. 'We'll keep those to show to
our children . . . and grandchildren,' he said.

'You seem very sure of yourself.' I had no intention of being
taken for granted.

'When you've been on the brink and back again, it gives you a new perspective . . . a more clearly defined outlook on the future. Don't you agree?'

I remained silent.

'The nurse told me you'd be in this afternoon.' He seemed unaffected by my lack of response.

'I wanted to see you so that I could sleep tonight,' I said.

'We didn't do badly, did we? Henry tells me that it is all but sewn up now. A pity that much of the story will never be told.'

'I can't help wondering where Peter fitted in,' I said, watching for his reaction.

'What makes you suspect that Peter might be involved?'

'He has to be in there somewhere. But, on which side?' I said. 'Barry was cagey, but he dropped a vague hint. I think Henry was afraid I might do some digging on my own. He told me Peter had arrived back in the UK early yesterday, and had returned to New York on the same flight that Barry took last night. I tried a little probing, but I might have saved my time. He simply warned me to keep my mouth shut.'

'You must do just that.' It was an order, not a suggestion. 'It seems a pity that you won't get the credit for what you did last night,' he said, steering the conversation in another direction. 'Those involved are the only ones who will know how you saved the operation from being a complete disaster.'

'I recognized Smith, and I rang a church bell. Big deal!' I said. 'But, Barry saved us both, and what sort of acknowledgement will he get?'

'Public acclaim is the last thing he'd want.' Ian touched my fingers. 'Your hands . . . how much damage?'

'Nothing serious. I'm hoping to be able to drive by the end of the week. I can't ignore that I have a house restoration on my books: I've got to get down to work.'

He nodded. 'You know I'll be out of here tomorrow?'

'Yes. I plan to visit Harriet in the afternoon, and nobody's going to stop me this time. I'll see you there.' I glanced over my shoulder. 'The nurse is on her way to throw me out. I must go, or Kate will be on the war-path.'

He pulled me closer.

'How do I convince you that I'm in love with you?' he said, and his kiss, if nothing else, was adequate indication that he was making a swift recovery.

The following morning, I came down to earth, spending the time checking all my calculations, ringing the builders, and arranging to meet the owners of the house with the architect. The builders were ready to begin their work, and had agreed to start on the following Monday.

I had an 11.30 appointment at the hospital to have the dressings on my hands changed. Kate took me there, looking after me like a mother hen with a wayward chick.

'I haven't seen rope burns for some years,' the nurse said, 'but it looks as though you heal quickly. The pain should ease in a day or two. You're not attempting to drive, I hope?'

Kate chipped in, assuring her that I would not be driving until my hands had fully healed. I was beginning to understand why her own brood were living at a distance.

After a light lunch, all three of us took to the road, arriving at the cottage hospital in the early afternoon.

The consultant was with Ian, and so Maxwell, Kate and I were escorted to Harriet's room. She was fully dressed and sitting in an armchair near the window. Maxwell and Kate had never met her before. With introductions made, I told Harriet that she would be getting her valuables back in due course. I also gave her Barry's message, which she received with a nod of the head, but without comment.

190